Heart of
Onyx

Heart of Onyx

Cynthia Ayala

To order additional copies of this book, contact:
Xlibris Corporation
1-888-795-4274
www.Xlibris.com
Orders@Xlibris.com
74013

To my mother who figured out a way to get me to love reading and supporting me with all my craziness and who bought me all my composition books to write in. Love you mommy!

To all my friends, wish I could name you all, thanks for being around whenever I needed you. You're the best friends anyone could ask for.

To my teachers who helped me to become a better writer and who didn't mind when I wrote in class instead of taking notes.

Love you guys!

Chapter One

S elene sat near the crystal waif at the edge of her palace. The fish followed her skipping stone and she smiled and turned her head to her best friend. A princess and a servant boy. He was older than herself, she knew, but why should that interfere with their fun. She watched as he picked up a rock and threw it. The fish scattered then followed and she laughed. She looked at the crystal blue water and wondered what lay beyond her kingdom. Suddenly she had an impulse she needed to act on. Selene took off her shoes, and when Edel wasn't looking, pushed him along with herself into the clear water.

She looked at him through the last few rays of the setting sun. He turned to her and smiled and she smiled back. She looked at her palace. As the sun reflected off it. A grand ivory and gold tower . . .

*　　*　　*

Selene woke with a start. It was just a dream, a faint memory. She got up from her bed and looked to stare at her once home. The castle, that had once been ivory and gold and that had glistened with light, was how black and silver and shrouded in darkness. The land that once was green with life was now slowly dying away. She remembered the day she escaped and the castle was taken. Edel had helped her and now resided in the same village as she herself. The Evil Empress thought she was dead, and laid rotting away with the rest of her family.

Selene had watched as they were slain as she herself was forced to keep quiet. She has always wanted to escape the castle and wander around before taking up her proper place as King's Mage, but not in the way in which it had happened.

She had taken up the identity of a sorceress and at that thought, she smiled for she was becoming very good at it.

Selene walked amongst the towns people until she saw him. Edel stood by the fountain and stared at the dirty water that came from the spout. She tapped him on his shoulder and he just stared at her.

"Hello Selene," he said calmly.

"Hello Edel." She looked around. "I take it the towns people need water?"

He nodded solemnly. "You know the only clean water flows only at the once known crystal waif."

Selene laughed harshly. "The crystals that are now onyx stone, poisoned with evil." She turned toward him, her face impassive. "Edel we can*not* live like this any longer. She must be stopped."

He stared down at her angrily. "And how do you plan to destroy her?" he asked harshly, making her flinch. She had never seen him this angry. "You can't just walk in and fight her and hope that she is weak! You don't know enough spells."

"So your saying that if I knew more spells I would be able to defeat her?"

"No, but you *would* be able to drain her, making her weak. She's pure evil if you haven't forgotten, as well as immortal," he added sadly. He paused a moment, his face growing soft again. "Which stories about her becoming what she is now do you believe?"

"The one I believe to be true. How she was a mage, who fell in love, but when he, whoever he was, didn't love her back, gave herself to the dark magic when she became distraught. Now no one can resist her and when she sinks those black talon nails of hers into you, all you will ever know again is hatred and loathing and anger and anything else you can throw into that sad."

Selene felt her body jerk when she heard him laugh. She hadn't heard him laugh like that in years. Selene promised herself that she would ask him why the cause for laughter in such a dire situation, but right now the people were counting on her to purify the water. The fountain glowed at the end of her simple yet powerful spell. They were lucky if this lasted a week. She began walking away from the fountain and glared at the palace. One day, she swore as she did every day since her escape, she would face her families killer and destroy her.

* * *

They were kissing. She had been gone for weeks and they didn't care that she was gone, or that she might be dead. He was a thief, her best friend, the love of her life. She was a puny princess with no knowledge of magic, a pathetic mage. She shut her eyes and cried against the boulder that protected her existence. It wasn't fair. She loved him, always had, he should love her back, she thought he did. Her anger grew, with each passing minute as well as her heart ache and with each minute that passed she wanted revenge more and more. Then *he* came, evil incarnate, the one she had come on this journey to stop. Luciana stood, tears streaming down her cheeks.

"What do you want?" she demanded.

He stood there with his arms open. "I can feel your anger Luciana. Come and I'll help you get your revenge. I can help you hurt them. All you need is my power and all will be granted."

She shook her head back and forth violently and placed her hands over her ears to block out his voice. This was just his essence; she had killed with her bears hands, turning him into what he was now. He could no longer do any harm. But still . . .

"No, I don't want to hurt him . . . I want to hurt her." Her eyes blazed with a fire that could not be extinguished, that pleased him.

"Then come to me."

She looked at him then back at her love with his lips pressed hard against the lips of that retched princess. Her hatred grew. She walked to him and he embraced her. He was nothing but a phantom and with his powers given to her, he was nothing.

Luciana opened her eyes and they turned cold and filled with hatred. Her robes, turned from a gleaming white to black. She looked at herself and an evil seducing smile crossed her face. She turned around and walked toward her old friends.

"Well I can see you didn't worry about me at all. Such loyal true friends you are, right Corbett?"

Corbett and the princess broke apart and stared at her in confusion and shock.

"Luciana?" asked Corbett.

Luciana smiled and spread her arms. "Yes Corbett it is I. Don't you love the new look I've chosen? I think it suits me more than the white. Oh and the Evil Lord is gone; I killed him. You can thank me later of course, but after I do what I'm about to do, you will be wanting to kill me."

"Luciana—"

"I'm sorry my love."

Luciana snapped her finger and everything dead arose from the ground. She pointed a finger at Corbett and the princess Nora.

"Kill them."

Luciana rose herself into midair and sat there amused, watching. She knew Corbett would live, it was the princess she was more concerned about. She looked around and swore when she didn't see her. Suddenly she sensed something coming her way and turned around. Luciana caught a ball of magic filled with light.

"Now, now princess, is this any way to treat a friend?"

Luciana sneered and crushed the ball, then summoned it whole again only with darkness inside of it. Nora gasped as the ball was thrown at her. She was trapped. Luciana began walked toward her when she felt the tip of a blade at the back of her neck.

"Let her go, Luciana." The blade inched closer.

"Fine . . . I will let her go."

Luciana snapped her fingers and the bubble turned back into an onyx crystal. Before they could embrace each other, Luciana grabbed Corbett's sword and thrust it through Nora from behind. She watched as Corbett stood stunned.

Luciana grabbed Nora's dying neck and sunk her black nails in. She knew that this would make Nora her un-dead minion.

"Goodbye Corbett. I'll see you soon."

She smiled and went to her black castle with Nora. Corbetts' priceless expression so vividly in her mind . . .

*   *   *

Luciana, the Dark Queen, blinked her eyes. Her memories of centuries ago still haunted her. The fight, the battle, all of it she remembers so vividly. She traced the white scars on her body. She stood and stared at her reflection.

"Oh sweet Corbett, you should have killed me that day while you still had the chance. Maybe all our friends wouldn't be my minions."

A knock came at the door and Luciana told whoever it was to come in. It was Nora. The cold dead angry blue eyes were still as elegant as ever.

"More thieves have been captured Luciana, but none of them are Corbett."

Luciana laughed and looked at her briefly, amused. "Silly Nora, do you really think he'd be a thief? No, I've been sensing magic from the village. He might have taken the identity of a mage." She laughed again.

"I don't see what's so funny."

"I think he's trying to defeat me by the use of magic." She stared at her reflection and glared down at herself.

Nora walked over to Luciana and handed her cloak. Luciana put it on and grabbed her sword. She masked her face in a black cloud. She stood there a moment before changing her mind. Everyone knew that to look upon her face was to look upon death.

They walked through the hallways of the palace. Luciana was growing irritated by Nora's stare and stopped.

"What is it already?"

"Why do you think he's using magic to defeat you?"

""I sense magic in the town. Magic being used to *help* the people. I sense *him*."

Nora looked at her thoughtfully. "Maybe, but these thieves have taken his name. Maybe they do that to mock you."

"Then I will kill them . . . slowly."

They entered the Grand Hall in which she liked to keep her prisoners held. She walked in and saw the thieves on their knees tied. They looked up slowly at her. Their faces froze in terror as they looked upon her face.

"Hello thieves. I'm going to ask you a couple of questions and you're going to answer them. Then, you're all going to die . . . slowly." She smiled and walked toward them.

* * *

He saw his friends, one by one getting slaughtered and becoming *her* minions. He turned around and quickly destroyed another un-dead soldier. He looked around again and his eyes stopped at Nora as she stabbed her sword through her brother. He suddenly felt a sharp tip against his neck.

"Hello my love."

He turned around slowly and faced her. He hated looking at her. He had loved her once and that was why he hated her so much.

He swung his sword at her and she dodged easily. They fought and fought, and soon enough he began to win. He kicked her down and tapped her at the side of her stomach. He pulled it out slowly and stared down at her. She rocked back and forth and was muttering something incoherent. He leaned his head forward to hear her better.

"No one loves me . . . no one cares." He shook his head in disgust.

"We cared once Luciana! You know that!" He sheathed his sword and stood straight. "I'll let you live Luciana, only so you can die in loneliness."

11

He watched her confused as she began laughing uncontrollably. She stared up at him as tears froze upon her skin.

"Don't you understand, Corbett," she ended in disgust. "I can't die! I'm immortal! I killed the Dark Lord and when he gave himself to me, he cast a spell! Only I know it Corbett! You can't destroy me and when you die I will still be here!"

Corbett watched as his friend raised herself into the air.

"Right now though, Corbett, you probably could've killed me." She laughed. "You should've killed me while you had the chance."

She disappeared, along with her newfound minions, in a cloud of black smoke. Corbett stood before turning and running toward Nora's brother to examine the wound. It wasn't a fatal wound, but he had fallen unconscious. He looked around, including himself, there were only five survivors. They walked to him and knelt down by his side.

"I had the chance to kill her and I didn't take it."

"It's not your fault, Corbett," soothed his friend Isabelle. He looked at her wide, sad green eyes. "She used to be our friend . . . my sister for years."

She hugged him and they all sat around their prince. Suddenly a white glow appeared and they saw a woman walking toward them.

"Who are you," demanded Corbett pulling out his sword.

"I am the equal to the dark mage. But as they go, so must I, but I have a proposition for you." Corbett stared at her. Sadness marked her face.

"What is it?"

"As he became one with her, I will become on with all of you. But you must keep your identities secret. When the time comes, you all will fight her and I warn you, choose your companions carefully for that task. Right now, she is weak and is in hiding, learning and preparing herself for that day. Immortality is now yours, as it is hers."

She disappeared and Corbett closed his eyes as white light engulfed them. He opened his eyes and saw Nora's brother awaken from his unconsciousness.

"What happened," he asked groggily.

"A lot," answered Corbett sadly as he stared up at the fortress.

*   *   *

Corbett opened his eyes and looked up from his drink. The time was here, he would feel it within the webs of magic. He had to find his old friends and hopefully his new companions and theirs, were the right people for this task.

He looked around for the town mage. She stood at the bar and looked at him. A warm smile lit her face. He thought that she and her friends were a good choice, he only hoped that he wasn't wrong.

.

Chapter Two

Selene woke up with Edel holding her. She looked up at him and noticed that he was still fast asleep. They lay together in the green meadow under a large oak tree. For some reason all land east of the River of Darkness was kept green and beautiful. The "queen" liked it that way.

She rustled his black hair and woke him up. He blinked a few times as though remembering his surrounds and looked at her. She smiled warmly at him and he smiled back. He was different, she thought. She and her companions were going to stop her majesty but they needed more people to even try to get past her vast army and defeat her.

Their friend Arlis had suggested that they leave North to the true castle of the queen. The Fortress. Everyone knew that she always went back there. Her memories haunted her, which she often made clear for all to see.

Edel sat up and rubbed his eyes. She watched as he stared sadly at the castle.

"Why do you look so sad?"

He laughed and looked at her. "It's sad how all have suffered for ones' mistake. Who knew that love was such a powerful thing."

Selene agreed and sat back once again. She stared deeply into the sky and noticed the time. It was nearing dusk.

"When should we leave Edel?"

"In a few days that should give us the time we need to prepare ourselves for the journey ahead."

Selene agreed once again and looked toward the palace, her home, once upon a time.

Luciana had come and killed her family one by one in dark delight right in front of her face. She herself would have died if Edel had not grabbed her and kept her safe behind a thick tapestry. Selene remembered hiding with Edels' hand over her mouth hushing her as her little brother was stabbed before her eyes without a second thought.

"I'll stop her."

"I hope you can," was his solemn reply.

*   *   *

Luciana examined the dead bodies, seeing if they were fit to become part of her ever growing legion. They weren't exactly physically fit, but they were good archers, that much she had confirmed as she pulled a few arrows from her throat, neck and chest.

"Luciana, just go ahead and add them already," said Nora rather annoyed.

Luciana looked at her agitated, things were on her mind. "You do it, I need to retire." Luciana smiled serenely and walked off to her room. She leaned against the door and stared around her room. Empty and alone, just like Corbett had promised.

"Damn you Corbett." She walked over to her mirror and punched it. Soon enough Luciana was tearing apart her room, slashing her curtains and bed sheets, tearing everything into pieces here and there. She finally stopped and sat on her bed, her dishevelled hair covering her face, making her angelic face look deranged. Hatred fuelled her anger and she began to laugh hysterically.

"Have you finally lost your damn mind," said Nora calmly standing at the door.

"No, I'm just reminiscing." She looked at Nora who's hand happened to be on the hilt of her sword. It seemed to always be like that now and days. Luciana often wondered if she could also feel what was coming.

"I think you've lost your mind," said Nora quite bluntly.

Luciana smiled slightly. "Glad to know you kept your sense of humour these past few centuries."

"Me too. Now tell me . . . why haven't your wounds healed?"

"I don't know," said Luciana growing angry.

Nora walked to her side and drew out her sword. Luciana stared at it, fully knowing what Nora intended, so Luciana just stood up, took a step back and opened her arms wide. Nora's sword cut deeply into her skin.

"You're wounds aren't healing?" asked Nora examining her wounds.

"I don't know, I think maybe my immortality might just be running out." She smiled.

"How can you find this amusing?"

"I've lost my mind remember."

Nora sheathed her sword and stared at her. So she could feel it, thought Luciana.

"You're getting rusty. You need to practice your swordsmanship."

Nora walked from the room and Luciana blinked away tears in disgust. She knew Nora was right. She disappeared in a black mist.

Their stronghold, where it all began. Luciana grabbed her sword from its place on the wall and walked to the lone mirror in the empty room. She called into the mirror and there he stood, her master.

"You called?"

"My immortality is running out. I need someone to practice my swordsmanship with." He nodded and walked from the mirror, a mist covered his hand as he summoned a sword.

"Fine then, let us begin."

They spared for the day without stopping once. Soon though, she finally began to grow weary and called to a halt.

"The day is approaching. I can feel it. My wounds, they aren't healing as fast as they used to." She looked up scared and angry. "What if he finds out how to kill me?"

H placed a cold misty hand on her shoulder. "He won't. He can't. Once he dies my dear, you will need to bear an heir. Your reign will last for all eternity."

"It had better."

She stood and walked to her room. She grabbed a single red rose and blew into it. The red darkened to black instantly.

"Find Corbett," she commanded before she blew the petals into the winds and collapsed onto her bed.

*　　*　　*

Corbett skulked around the forest. One of his old friends had come or a visit and was waiting.

"I am here Corbett." He looked up. There on a branch sat an elf girl.

"Come down here Trixie, it's difficult to talk to you when you're up in a tree."

"Fine," she groaned. Trixie jumped down landing gracefully on her feet. "It's nice to see you again Corbett."

"Same here." He gave her a warm hug then parted taking a step away from her. "How are you?" Corbett stressed the concern in his voice.

"Tired and hungry, we all are. How's Coryn?"

"He's fine." He looked around. "We have a set of fighters and we have changed our names. Has Isabelle told you that?"

Trixie shook her head. "I've barely talked to her. If it weren't for you sending letters to us all, I wouldn't be here, and none of us would be regrouping." She looked at him thoughtfully. "What are the names Corbett."

"The ones 'she' gave us," he said solemnly. He had expected a slap but none came.

"Why on earth would you do a stupid thing like that," she asked in disgust.

"Because . . . we just did all right. Don't question us, more importantly don't question me."

"Fine." Trixie shook her head and muttered something in elvish as she began rummaging in her bag. Corbett knew it would be stupid to ask so he just stood there, an arms length away.

Trixie pulled out a piece of parchment and handed it to him. He took, a questioning look upon his face. Without worry though he opened it and looked at her.

"A map?"

"Yes. You see over here, that is where my band and I will meet you."

"I would prefer you act like you don't know me."

"I . . . will try."

"Good." He looked back down at the map and his eyes widened. "Trixie that's at least a months journey from here!"

"Oh hush, whining doesn't become you." She paused and looked at him sadly. "We all miss her Corbett."

He gripped the map hard and stared at her scornfully. "I don't miss her!"

"No but you once loved her. I will leave you to your solitude now. See you in a month." She stepped up to him and kissed him on the cheek before walking away.

Corbett stood and waited till she was far gone before he began to punch into a tree. He soon fell to the ground, crying out in anguish. He didn't care that his hands were blistered ad bleeding, he just cared about her.

*　　*　　*

Selene laid on her bed and stared at the ceiling. Soon, she promised herself, soon. Suddenly, her window jerked open and something flew in and landed on her forehead. She swatted at it and stared at a black petal that was on her pillow.

"Oh god." Her pillow began turning black and soon enough the blackness began to spread onto her sheets. Selene jumped out of bed and searched for her ball of light. When she found it she thrust it onto her bed, stopping the darkness at the foot of her bed. She slunk to the floor and waited.

The door flew open and at the threshold stood Edel and their friend Arlis. They looked at the bed then at her. She smiled weakly at them. Edel ran to her and Arlis quickly closed the door.

"Nice of you to stop by, late as it is."

"Are you all right," asked Ede.

"I'm fine. Can we please focus on getting rid of my tainted bed." She looked over at Arlis who was holding a rolled piece of paper.

"Arlis, what's that?"

"A map. Now after this I take it, we will be leaving sooner than planned."

"Arlis, shut up and help with the sheets," demanded Edel. He turned back towards Selene. "Are you sure you're all right?" Selene nodded.

She stood behind them and watched as they lit the sheets on fire. The sheets burned away and vanished. It never even spread from the bed, she noticed.

"Well that's taken care of. Come on gather over here."

"Arlis, how can you act like nothing happened?" yelled Edel.

"I will, after we focus on where we are travelling."

Edel and Selene exchanged a look before walking toward Arlis who was already smoothing the map on the floor before him. Selene sat down next to Edel and craned her neck to see the map clearer.

"We are going here," he said indicating far off point. "That's the palace. Do you remember the place you fled to?"

"Yes, it was a tavern. I remember it, the tavern owner, um what was her name again Edel?"

"Isabelle I think."

"Ah yes. We ran far away, tell we got there. She's the one who gave me the spell books. She said her sister no longer had any use for them." The sentence stung Corbett.

"Really?" Arlis' eyes flashed back and forth between Edel and Selene. "Well, we're going there, maybe we can . . . gather more companions on our way."

Selene scrunched her eyes in wonder in the way he finished his sentence.

"All right, agreed," stated Edel. Now Arlis, Selene will be sleeping at my house, I think she will be safer."

"All right, I'm tired anyway. I've had a rough day see you later. Anyway I have to meet someone and I'm already running late. Take care Selene." He kissed her lightly on the cheek before stalking out.

"Edel, do you know what's wrong with him?"

"No, he's been acting like that all day. It's starting to get a bit irritating if you ask me." Selene laughed and Edel smiled. "It's nice to see you smiled again."

"It feels nice to smile. I actually feel happy."

"Come on let's get going. Grab your books and some clothes okay. I'll . . . keep a look out outside if that makes you feel better."

"It would, thank you."

"I'm always at your service . . . princess." He bowed and walked out, closing the door behind him. Selene just stood there staring at the door. At least I'm still a princess to someone, she thought blissfully.

She smiled and grabbed her books and some clothes. She stopped at her window and took one last perfect view of her once beautiful palace and home.

"One day," she said as she turned away and walked out into the arms of Edel.

Chapter Three

Luciana called forth her most faithful minions, her only *true* friends. Nora stood at the front of the small group and pulled forth her sword. The rest followed suit.

"Whatever it is you have to say, say already, I grow bored," said Luciana picking her nails.

"I will go first," said Nora. "I feel it. Immortality is fading. I vote we find them and kill or torture them till they die first."

"I second that," said Esmeralda stepping forth, her elf ears highlighting her marble features. "We should kill them, do everything in our power to do so."

"I'm not so sure I agree," said Nathaniel.

Luciana eyed him curiously. "Why?"

"Because, we can't risk it, we need an army. We know that they are gathering an army, and their immortality is also fading we have the upper hand, and we can't risk losing it just to torment and kill. They could escape, so we need a vast army to secure our victory."

"That's too obvious though. They all know us far too well. They will anticipate that," said Daniel, Luciana's favourite half-elf thief as he fingered his black dagger.

"I have something better. We do nothing. We watch then come out and tell my lovely tragic story. In that time being we take one of their men, or many, and turn them till they feel sympathy for me and kill them off . . . one by one." Luciana smiled.

"That sound like a brilliant idea," said Adira. "One flaw though: we don't know who they are."

"Wrong. Supposedly, the princess is still alive and like all princesses, she will have a weak spot for my story, no offense Nora."

"None taken." She paused her cold eyes searching the ground thoughtfully. "Do you think that Corbett has fallen for her?"

"I think he will try to keep his attention away from princesses; that is after all what got him into this mess in the first place. No offense Nora," said Entia stifling her laughter.

"None taken," said Nora drenching each word with hostility.

"Luciana, do you think they know your sister," asked Damien.

"Who cares about her," said Nathaniel. Luciana looked at him. He was fingering an arrow withered with age. Luciana looked into his eyes when he looked up. They shared a similar pain.

"Enough! No more talk about those people. Everyone go, hang about, torment people, act normal for all I care, just find out what you can and leave . . . NOW!" They all obeyed without question and once the door was closed, Luciana crumbled to the ground. All her memories flooded her mind and she could no longer fight them off as she had over the past six centuries.

"Luciana," said Corbett. She looked at her long-time friend and stood up. They were at the kingdom looking for more companions to join their fight. Her little sister Isabelle, had already found some and was already taking a liking to a fine young man who shared her interest in archery.

Luciana got up and wiped her wet hands on her white robe to dry them. "Yeah?"

"I think I found some more companions."

"Really, who?"

"The princess and prince." Corbett smiled his crooked smile that made her just want to grab and kiss him, but at this moment she was trying to comprehend what he had just said.

"Your kidding right? What use could they be?"

"Come on Luci, we need all the help we can, besides the princess can do magic and the prince can fight."

"The question now is can she perform magic?" She was becoming irritated. Luciana didn't feel like the prince and princess could be any help, she knew they would slow them down.

"I don't know, that's why I came for you." He smiled again and this time she couldn't resist so she shrugged. What harm could it be? She asked herself.

"Fine then, let's go before I change my mind." Corbett grin widened whilst she rolled her eyes, even though, despite herself, she smiled.

Corbett grabbed her around her waist and pulled her along. Luciana looked up at his warm face and wished he knew how she truly felt.

Luciana jerked her eyes open when a dagger landed in the ground in front of her.

"Why do you still love him," asked Damien summoning his dagger back to his hand.

"Because I do," she said holding back the tears. "Now leave me."

*　*　*

Selene was tired do to the fact that she had barely slept in three days. She looked around her friends for Arlis. As always, he stood alone, away from the crowd. Selene got up from her seat and walked over to him.

"Arlis are you all right?"

"You watched your family die yet you are . . . not such an angry person."

Selene shrugged. "I don't want to be angry like her, so I try not to let my anger consume me."

"Smart."

"Did you lose someone?"

"I lost many."

"I'm so sorry." Selene saw the sadness crawl over his face. "Anyway, these friends, can we trust them?"

"Completely, don't worry." He finally looked down at her, a smile delicately painted on. "So, are you and Edel serious?"

Selene was caught off guard and looked over at Edel quickly. He was leaning against a tree with that thoughtful expression on his face.

"I'm not sure, to tell you the truth. I love him, but then again he saved my life."

He nodded and looked at her. "True. Well get back to sleep."

She nodded. It wasn't her time to keep watch but it might as well be since she couldn't sleep but maybe now she might be able to.

"All right Arlis." She kissed him lightly on the cheek and went back to bed.

Selene was shaken. After hiding in her village a guy Arlis said they should run away. He had said he knew of a place they could hide out. Edel had cared for her, hugged and was just there for her whenever she needed a shoulder to cry on. She had always loved him, but now, she loved him more than ever.

When they had reached the tavern he had sat her down and went to find the owner Arlis had told them about. He had returned with Isabelle. She was gentle and gave her comfort as well as a room and a couple old advanced spell books. Apparently the Dark Queen took her sister said she no longer had any use for them. Selene had loved every minute of planning revenge and being with Edel.

*　　*　　*

Corbett was stuffing down food with no regard. He finally looked up and saw the princess sitting uncomfortably in the dirty tavern. He stifled a laugh and looked at her brother. He was actually getting along with the thugs. Again Corbett stifled a laugh.

He looked around for Luciana. She was throwing darts with amazing accuracy, pounding the bull's-eye each and every time. He looked her up and down and realized that for once she was not wearing her white robes and instead looked more like a thief.

Luciana was angry, he knew, after all the princess wasn't her favourite person. Luciana suddenly stopped and looked at him angrily before stalking out of the tavern. He swallowed down his food and was about to go talk to her when something inched into the back of his neck. He knew it was an arrows head.

"Sit Corbett," ordered Isabelle.

"Fine, but can you please put the arrow away."

"As you wish." She did and sat across from him, her eyes digging their way into him like Luciana's did whenever she was doing magic, only he knew Isabelle couldn't, she never tried.

"Do you like Nora?"

"No . . . well maybe e a little, but it's not a big deal. She's a princess and I'm nothing and when all this is over it'll be like I never existed." Why did I just tell her that, Corbett asked himself. Isabelle sighed and looked at him sadly her eyes no longer frightening.

"You're an ignoramus."

"Why?"

"Correct that, an oblivious ignoramus."

"Why? Does Nora like me?"

An expression of frustration coloured her face. "No, but Luciana does. I swear you are like a child."

"Luciana? No, we've known each other for forever, she can't love me."

"I said like not love." Isabelle stopped rolling her eyes and looked at him shocked. "You have noticed!"

"Shut up, we're friends, that's it all right," he hissed.

"Whatever, do what you will. I'm going to go finish her game of darts." She smiled a Barmecidal smile when she got up and walked away, but Corbett heard her mutter, "why she wastes her time with you I'll never know."

Corbett ignored her as he walked outside. He saw Luciana, his Luci, standing by a tree braiding her long raven black hair. He stepped on a twig and swore, he wanted to surprise her, but she heard and turned around towards him, her jade eyes sparkling.

"Hi."

"Hi. Are you all right?"

"I'm fine, you?"

"Fine." He looked around. "What are you doing out here?"

Her eyes turned cold. "Getting away from that stupid princess who can't even mutter a single spell." Her eyes went back to their sparkling and Corbett smiled. "She's useless. I swear it's a good thing she's a princess or I would have never agreed to this."

"Come on, don't be so harsh on her." Luciana glared at him but he smiled and place his hands on her shoulders. He watched her eyes begin to fill with love.

"Corbett, come on lets go back inside."

"Wait, it's nice out here, let's stay out a little while longer." Luciana smiled and finally consented.

"Okay, but just a while longer." He looked deep into her bright jade eyes glistened with love and he felt his own heart skip a beat. All of a sudden those same eyes were filled with fear.

"CORBETT!" He turned back. The dark lord was holding her. He fought away another dead minion and was about to go back for her. Something hit him and he flew to the ground. He stabbed his sword into the ground to keep from flying away.

"Corbett!"

"Luciana! I'll come back for you! I promise!" Then he flew out the great black doors no longer able to hold on.

Corbett opened his eyes. He could still remember her. He had broken the promise he had made. Maybe he could save her, maybe he could find a spell to rid her of him. He remembered when he had fought her. Her eye and nails where black as stone. He would never admit it aloud, but he missed her, in fact he loved her and that was why he hated her so.

"Hey Corbett," he heard someone whisper. He knew it was Trixie. He snuck away and shook Coryn awake. They both snuck off.

24

"Hey Trixie," they both said.

"Hi, how are you both?"

"Fine," said Coryn.

"Dealing," replied Corbett. "Hey, if you can be with her every night why can't you just bring your people?"

"Because it would be too much of a hassle. Now I have two mage's, how 'bout you?"

"The princess."

Trixie shot Corbett a look of bewilderment.

"Oh god no, that's what got us into all this mess."

"She's good at magic don't worry."

"I hope you're right. If Luciana ever finds out you're in deep shit."

"No I'm not, now shut up about her. Besides I'm going to kill her."

"How can you and Isabelle be so cold? She was once our friend. Why do you want to kill her so bad?" Trixie stared at him sadly, confused.

"Trixie look around," he said waving his hands around. "She causes nothing but pain. She's evil and deserves death."

"That maybe true but we're to blame for this as well. If we had gone back to see if she was alive instead of assuming and going on with our lives, none of this would be happening."

He looked at her opprobriously. "If I had just killed her when I had the chance, none of this would be happened."

She reproached his contempt for himself and her. "But you couldn't. I don't think any of us could. Isabelle could have shot an arrow a mile away into her heart but she didn't. We all are were given a chance to kill her and none of us took that chance."

"Can I change the subject," said Coryn timidly. "Do you think Nathaniel still loves Isabelle?"

"Isn't he the General with a withered arrow as his symbol," asked Trixie. Coryn nodded. "Than yes."

"Do you think Isabelle cares?" asked Corbett.

"No. Nora bears the royal symbol encased in blood, do you care Coryn?"

"Yes and it makes me sick."

"Then that's how Isabelle feels. Look, I must get back to my men, I will see you soon." She smiled and then ran off.

"Corbett, do you think we will have to kill all of them? Do you think that there is really no way to save them?"

"They're dead Coryn, there is no way to save any of them." Corbett fingered his dagger.

"Luciana's not dead, just weak and slightly possessed."

"I'm going back to sleep." Corbett was sick of hearing about Luciana. To him, she was dead.

Chapter Four

Corbett was tired. They needed horses to cover more ground. According to the map there was a town just a couple more miles east. Someone tapped his shoulder. He turned around startled only to realize that it was only Selene.

"Hey."

"We need to rest." He looked into her blue eyes.

"There's a town nearby, I was thinking we could buy a couple horses, rest up and gather more companions." He smiled down at her.

"I guess, but we must hurry, I think we all are ready to collapse." She laughed and stopped suddenly.

"What's wrong?" he asked.

"Someone's coming down the road. Everyone get off the road!" Everyone obeyed without question and hid in the thick brush surrounding the road.

Corbett watched and his breath. It was Esmeralda, Trixie's sister. Her chestnut hair was fixed neatly up. She stopped her calvary and got own off her black horse. Behind her, her calvary stood holding up her banner, her symbol. As an elf of royal blood her symbol was of a tree dead and on barren land. She looked around suspiciously, cautiously; her elven ears twitched her and there to hear better.

"General Esmeralda?" asked one of her men.

"It's nothing, I thought I sensed . . ." she smiled, "an old friend." She turned and got back on her horse, her symbol wavering on her cape and glistening on her breast plate in the sun. Esmeralda galloped off and her calvary followed suit. Corbett looked at Coryn, they would have to keep a low profile.

"Selene, get everyone ready, we're heading to the village."

"But . . ."

"Selene trust me." She nodded and gathered everyone up.

"Corbett, she's going to recognize us."

"No she won't, not if we keep hidden."

"I hope you're right."

"Yeah, me too."

*   *   *

Luciana was walking around searching for Corbett. She knew where he was, but it was taking her a while to get to him. She had to shove through the people in her village. Chaos was everywhere, deaths and loss. Everything was becoming torn. Soon in the forest she found hm. Luciana couldn't bear to see Corbett crying. She looked at the ground as she approached him and leaned on his shoulder.

"Corbett?"

"What?" he said harshly.

"Are you all right?"

"What do you think."

"I know it was a stupid question." She tilted her head up and looked up at him. He in turn looked down at her. Both of his parents were just killed in the plague caused by the Evil Lord and neither her parents or her were able to save him.

"No, it's all right, you only care." He stopped and sighed. "He has to be stopped."

"Yes . . . oh no Corbett, you don't plan to be the one to do it do you."

"Yes I do. I'm going to use all my talents and I swear I'll kill him."

"If you insist then, but I'm coming as well."

"No you're not."

"Yes I am. If you think I'm going to let my oldest and best friend face evil alone, you must be insane. Besides, your talents alone won't be enough." She smiled and he hugged her tightly.

"I can always count on you Luci."

"I hope I can say the same."

"You know you can." Luciana returned the hug.

They were fighting their way in. Luciana was killing the un-dead again and again with blasts of magic. Corbett grabbed her and pulled her along after him. He fought another dark minion and Luciana looked around. The Dark Lord was staring at Corbett and preparing to shoot at him. She quickly pushed him out of the way and he fell down the stairs. The spell hit her and she fell to the ground. Luciana tried to get up, but whatever spell it was had made her weak. She was pulled up roughly and holding her was the Dark Lord. Luciana tried to pull away but he was to strong and held her tightly now with both of his arms. He began to pull away, and now she knew her feeble struggles would be in vain.

"Corbett!"

"Luciana!" She watched him try to come for her.

"Corbett!"

"Luciana! I'll come back for you, I promise!" Then he was gone, blown away with the dark magic as she was dragged to the dungeon. He never came.

Luciana waited for Esmeralda to report back to her. She was in the dungeon that he had put her in and tortured her in for weeks. Corbett never came, like she thought he would.

"Luciana." She knew it was Nora. She turned around and watched as a look of affrighting became painted on her face.

"What?"

"Oh my god."

"WHAT IS IT?!"

"Your eyes are green."

"WHAT!!" Luciana stormed from the dungeon and transported herself to her bedroom. Luciana walked to her mirror and stared at her disturbing reflection.

"Luciana your nails." She looked down at her nails. The black was fading away.

"He's losing control. He's losing his power. Magic and immortality is fading. I need an heir."

"This is not good."

"I know. Ugh finally, they are turning black again."

"Luciana I think there is more to this."

"Like what?"

"I think you are having a heart again."

"Don't say such horrid things, just go and catch up with Esmeralda."

"As you wish."

Luciana reverse the illusion spell and sighed. Her green eyes stared back at her. She gripped her nails into the dresser. Her hatred was still there, but love was clouding her thoughts.

"Damn you Corbett."

* * *

Selene was happy to be in a bed. Almost two weeks on the road with about fifteen people to feed and keep warm was becoming stressing and tiresome. Everyone was eating while she was resting. They were going to buy horses and supplies till they reach the next village. Selene plucked her head out from under the covers when someone knocked on her door.

"Come in."

A girl came in, her friend Artemisa who was mightily talented at swordsmanship. Her blond hair was short and her hazel eyes showed concern.

"Hello Artemisa."

"Selene, you are awake. How are you?"

"Tired, yourself?"

"Famished, yet satisfied." She smiled. "Arlis is worried that you straining yourself."

"I am, I need to rest." A galloping sounded and there was silence. Selene and Artemisa looked at each other before walking to the window. Outside was another female general who bored the royal symbol encased in blood.

"How dare she wear *my* symbol," hissed Selene.

"I think that is the General Nora. She is supposed to be the princess form the tales. They say she's the Queens most loyal minion."

"I thought all the Generals were."

"They are, but she was the first."

"Come on; let's go see what's going on."

"You've gone mad."

"I want to see if they will give us any idea of what they plan to do."

"Okay, I'll come with you." Selene smiled and got dressed.

Artemisa and her walked out ad down the stairs. Edel was picking up plates and helping out the owner. He turned, smiled and walked toward her.

"Hey, are you all right?"

"Fine. Artemisa and I are going to eavesdrop on the Generals."

"Generals?"

Selene nodded. "General Nora just arrived."

"What?" asked Arlis incredulously.

"General Nora, she's here."

Arlis ran up to his room and Selene stared after him. She turned to Edel and gave him a questioning glance.

"Edel?"

"I'll talk to him later, right now if you want free room and food, I have I work." He kissed her forehead and she looked at him. He looked like her servant boy again.

Selene walked from the inn and walked around to General Nora who was already talking to General Esmeralda.

"I told her I would call for her."

"Time is of the essence Esmeralda."

"I sensed Corbett on the road. I also sensed Coryn and Trixie. At least two of them are here."

"And you thought not to call her for that? Her senses are stronger, she can find out who is here."

"Do you think we should call for her?"

"In a minute. Someone is watching us. I think Corbett and my little brother sensed me and are watching."

Esmeralda smiled. "Now?"

Nora smiled in return and nodded. "Yes."

"Luciana, we sense Corbett."

Selene and Artemisa looked up from their hiding spot. Who was Corbett? Suddenly, the air stilled and the place grew dark, cold, and silent as though all like was gone. She looked up at the storm clouds that covered the land, but her eyes went to s beautiful woman in black. Luciana, the Dark Empress, had arrived. A malevolent smiled was on her face.

"You found Corbett?"

"Yes. He is somewhere in this village."

"Brilliant." She turned around with Nora and Esmeralda walked at her side. Nora and Esmerelda looked at each other puzzled. They went over to a Market stand. Selene and Artemisa watched in disgust and Luciana picked up and apple, turned it from bright red to black and stared at the young merchant.

"Does he look familiar to you two?" she heard Luciana ask.

"Corbett," they heard Nora say.

"Open your mouth," ordered Luciana. Selene watched as fear came across his face as he obeyed unwillingly. Luciana smiled and stuck the apple into his mouth. Slowly the blackness spread from the apple to the man.

"Oh my god," gasped Artemisa. They watched in horror as the young man fell to the ground dead, then rose back up, now un-dead.

"He's part of mine," said Nora quickly.

"What?! No fair," exclaimed Esmeralda. Selene looked back at Luciana she was rubbing her eyes.

"Nora, my eyes, are they green again."

"Yes."

"Good. I need them to be for what I am about to do." Selene and Artemisa exchanged worried looks. "Corbett! I know you're watching me! Oh Corbett darling please do stop hiding!" She paused. "Fine, leave me, you were always good at that! Look into my eyes Corbett! Look at them!!! What do you see? Oh Corbett all this is your fault! Oh, by the way . . . I know that your darling princess LIVES!! I know she lives Corbett so do tell me what are you going to do? Make the same mistake twice?" She laughed heartlessly. "Goodbye for now my love!" He eyes turned black.

Luciana, Nora and Esmeralda stood together, their backs to the forest and Selene sensed something. She looked toward the forest and saw three arrows shoot from it toward them. They all turned and caught the arrows with their fingers, snapping them in annoyance. Their faces amused yet annoyed.

"Esmeralda, keep an eye on the place for just a while longer. He can't hide forever," ordered Luciana.

"As you wish Luciana." Luciana disappeared leaving the cold darkness behind, and Nora rode off with her new footman.

"I wonder who Corbett is?" asked Artemisa.

"Me too." Selene was shaky. The Queen knew she was alive.

*　　*　　*

Corbett stared out the window. He had looked into her eyes and what he saw was not the dark Queen but instead his friends, the girl he had loved. He couldn't help but think that maybe he could find a way to save her. His words still rung in his ears after all these centuries. He had promised and never went back; he clenched his fist.

"Corbett, she knows Selene is alive. It was the black petal that she sent. What are we going to do?"

"Those were Trixies' arrows," he said ignoring the question. Corbett sighed. "We are going to have to lie low before we leave. She can't know it's us, that we are here."

"But . . . okay, but your whole plan confuses me sometimes. I mean I often forget who I am."

Corbett nodded in agreement. " So do I sometimes. Come on, let's just keep an eye on the princess."

Coryn nodded and got up from his seat. Once he was gone Corbett remembered that she had sacrificed herself to save him.

"Luciana . . . I'm sorry."

"Corbett . . ." Luciana stared out her bedroom and spoke his name after hearing him. She smiled happily and looked down at the white rose in her hand. " . . . I love you."

Corbett heard her and closed his eyes. He would not say it, not aloud.

Chapter Five

S elene mostly kept to her room during the rest of their duration of their stay. They knew she was alive. They knew and now General Esmeralda was looking for her as well as two men named Corbett and Coryn and a girl named Trixie. She was in danger. Who were these people, were they were the ones responsible for everything she was going through.

Someone knocked on her door and Selene jumped. "Selene . . ."

"Come in Edel." She sat up in bed and laid her head on her knees and she smiled at him.

"Are you all right?"

"They know I'm alive and this guy, Corbett, whoever he is, is ruining my life. He's watching me, I can feel it, and honestly I think he is amongst our ranks."

"What about this Coryn they're looking for? I mean id he is alive then that makes him your great-great-great . . . you know, he's your grandfather. Do you think he still lives, that is true?"

"I believe them." She looked into his eyes. "I looked into her eyes. For a moment she looked human, she looked like a sad hurt lost child. I pitied her." Edel gave her a shocked look that held an emotion Selene had never seen on his face.

"Wow, even after what she did to you?"

"I know, frightening isn't is."

He smiled at her and kissed her forehead. "It's cause you have a heart of pure gold now come, you need food."

"All right. Wait, are you working today?"

"Nope, the owner gave everyone a day off on account of the General."

"Understandable. Does that mean we have to pay for our rooms?"

"Arlis thinks that we should leave . . . today. We don't have that type of money and we already spent a lot on the supplies and horses."

"All right, I'll eat then pack."

Edel kissed her forehead again. "Good." Selene watched him leave and once the doors closed she pulled the covers her head. She didn't want to leave, she didn't want to do anything. She just wanted to hide. Finally though, she kicked off her covers, got dressed and snuck out the door. She walked down the stairs quickly and calmly. She spotted Edel and Artemisa sitting together along with Arlis and Blake. Selene looked at them both and they smiled at her. Edel and Artemisa got her attention when they smiled and waved at her.

"Finally she's awake," joked Artemisa. "For a moment I thought you might have died."

"Ha-ha funny. So what's to eat?"

"Nothing, just drinks. He doesn't have anybody to cook for him," said Edel.

"The poor guy," said Blake.

"You're telling me. It's a good thing the dead don't have to eat," said Arlis. "Makes me sick."

"I agree, now let's not talk about it," said Selene. They all nodded in agreement and she smiled.

The day passed slowly and they were all ready to leave at nightfall. Suddenly at Mid-day, the air stilled and everything grew quiet. Selene backed behind a wall.

"Hello Luciana."

"What is the problem Esmeralda?"

"I have not found Corbett and frankly I can't stay here any longer."

"Fine. One more day. If you find nothing level the town and kill everyone in it."

"Thank you."

"Anything for a friend." Selene watched as Luciana left. She had to tell everyone because if she didn't, they would all die, or worse, be turned.

*　*　*

Corbett had listened as Selene spoke. They had to get out now. He sat on his bed and looked at the map. They were going to have to cut through the woods. Best part about that is that it will cut down on time to meet Trixie. He snuck out to the stables and saw Coryn and Trixie waiting.

"I can't believe you shot at them," hissed Corbett as he approached.

"I didn't think they would sense the arrows."

Corbett looked at her in disbelief. This was Luciana they were talking about. "You could have destroyed everything we have worked for!"

"You let yourself be known!"

"You did that for me!"

"Enough you two! Look Trixie we are taking a detour, with that detour Corbett explained to me earlier, we should be able to meet you within a couple of weeks or so. What name are we to call you by?"

"Nila."

"Okay."

"I'm leaving now see you later," said Corbett.

He walked back through the stables followed by Coryn. Luciana knew she was alive. She knew Selene was alive.

"Luciana . . ."

"Corbett . . ."

He clenched his fist at her mocking tone. He still loved her but he would not let her know, he would not tell her to give her that satisfaction.

"Corbett, you need to calm down."

"Shut up Coryn. Look just get the horses ready all right."

"Yeah sure. Where are you going?"

"A walk."

"Corbett . . ."

Get the damn horses ready Coryn." This time Coryn didn't say anything. Corbett walked off and leaned against a tree. He was the cause of everything. Everything he tried to think of why he hadn't gone back it was a blur. He closed his eyes briefly and when he opened them back up, General Nora had a sword to his throat.

"You've been watching me?"

"You're not that special Corbett. But my, my, won't Luciana be happy tomorrow when Esmeralda brings you and your pathetic band of friends to the fortress. I think Luciana will put you in *her* dungeon." She laughed coldly.

He looked at her scrutinisingly. "You won't take the credit?"

"Like I said, you're not that special. Besides Esmeralda is more than qualified to bring you in. Say hello to my brother and descendant for me Corbett." She flicked her sword intentionally, cutting his chin and walked away from her cape flapping behind her, her symbol glowing ominously in the moonlight. Corbett took his dagger and stabbed it into the tree behind him. He was fed up with it all.

Corbett walked back to the stables where everyone was sure to be. He touched his chin. The cut had healed, but it had healed slowly. Obviously he knew Nora's nature for the visit; she wanted to see if his immortality was running out. That could only mean one thing and it bought a satisfied smile to his face. So was hers.

*　　*　　*

Luciana was awaiting Nora's return. She cloaked her face as she walked around her kingdom. People bowed in her presence as she walked to the fountain. This was where the people got their clean water. This was where the puny princess would cast her feeble magic.

"Luciana!"

"Yes Nora?"

"I found Corbett."

Luciana stared at Nora with expectation. "And?"

"And I left him in the hands of Esmeralda. I think he is planning on trying to sneak away. I've already alerted Esmeralda and her men, they are keeping their eyes wide open. They'll find them."

Luciana smiled as she poisoned the water with a single touch. Nora was always so sure of herself, it had always been a flaw of royalty.

"I think he will escape Nora."

Nora flinched at the comment and Luciana smiled. "Why?"

"Because," she said heading back to the palace, "he is Corbett and *we* have a battle to win." She snapped her finger and the water turned into a vile sticky liquid.

"You seem so sure," said Nora with a smile.

"He doesn't know the key to my destruction."

"Don't you think he can figure it out?"

"If he does, it will be far too late. Has Nathaniel located my dear little sister yet?"

"She wasn't hard to find. She goes by her name and has owned the tavern by the fortress for almost thirty years now."

"Hmpf . . . It was Trixie who shot those arrows at us wasn't it?"

"Her arrows are unmistakable. It was amusing how she thought she could kill us."

"Trixie is far smarter than that, she knew she would not have been able to. It was just a distraction to pull Corbett from me and to pull me from Coryn and the princess."

37

Nora nodded in understanding. "Has anyone found Donovan as of yet?" continued Luciana.

Nora made a sour face. "Adira is still looking for him. It is difficult for her. Whenever she thinks she has him, she does not."

"Elves, their hearing is superior, which makes it hard to track them. Adira is lucky she is an elf or she would never be able to find his trail." Luciana turned around so that her cloaked face faced Nora. "Did you remember to give Corbett my gift?" echoed Luciana's cold voice.

"I'm sure it has healed by now."

"Good, now come, let's go meet our friends and pay my little sister a visit."

Luciana uncloaked her face and smiled. Her eyes were constantly shifting from black to green; at times it was an advantage, at others it was a nuisance.

Luciana loved the effect her presence had on nature itself; the world seemed to stand still and darkness seemed to cover the world as it did her soul. She looked at Nathaniel with his arrow that Isabelle struck him with once upon a time.

"Hello Nathaniel." He looked at her whilst he put his withered arrow away.

"Luciana," he said smiling. "Coming to say hi to your wench of a little sister?"

She smiled. "I always wondered why she liked this place," she said looking over the dingy tavern in scrutiny. "I never liked it."

"She's alone. It seems my presence has frightened her customers she is not very pleased with me." He chuckled under his breath.

"Too bad for her," she said heatedly as she walked into the tavern.

"We're closed," said Isabelle behind the counter. Luciana smiled, sat down in a chair and laced her fingers over her crossed legs.

"We don't' care . . . sister dear."

Isabelle dropped a glass and looked around behind her. She quickly pulled out her bow and three arrows, each aimed at Nathaniel, Nora and Luciana.

"I told him to leave and he refused, but he's just one person so I don't really care that much. Hell, I wouldn't mind it if all the generals came here, but you! No freaking way am I going to deal with you, you evil witch!"

"Oh come now little sister dear we haven't seen each other in, oh, six hundred years, I think we are far overdue for a reunion."

"Get out of my tavern or I'll shoot." Isabelle pulled her arrows back.

"Go ahead. Much harm it will cause us Isabelle," taunted Nora.

Isabelle laughed scornfully. "To think, you two started out hating each other. Don't you think it's funny *Empress* Luciana, *Princess* Nora." Her tone dripped cynicism.

"Don't you love us anymore?" asked Nathaniel scoffingly.

"I did, once, but no longer." She paused and all the hatred was gone, replaced with sadness. "Now get out of here before I waste my arrows."

"Fine," said Luciana standing up from her seat, "we will leave, but keep this in mind, little sister dear, I know the little Princess Selene lives."

Isabelle directed all three of her arrows into Luciana chest. Luciana smiled and walked over to the bar. One by one she calmly took an arrow out and placed it on the counter.

"Here, I know you're going to need all the arrows you can spare. Goodbye little sister." Luciana left the tavern and went back to her fortress.

"Well that was rather fun," she said as she poured herself, Nora and Nathaniel glasses of wine.

"I'll say," said Nora appearing in her black mist. Nathaniel laughed and Nora followed suit. Luciana simply smiled and leaned against the wall as she stared into her wine.

"Show me Corbett." The wine shifted and her reflection was replaced by Corbett on horseback. She blew into it to make it go away and noticed that once again, her eyes were green.

Chapter Six

S elene sat on her horse with her arms around Edel. They were sneaking out into the dead of night and she was using all her strength to keep them all invisible. She felt awful, leaving the village to burn but if she stayed and fought, she would no doubt be captured and then there would be no one who would be able to stop Luciana.

"Halt! Your invisibility spell may be able to fool my men but I am a general as well as an elf." Selene turned around, General Esmeralda was staring straight at her, smiling arrogantly.

"Come off that horse princess, her majesty would like a word with you. Mainly due to the fact that you seem as to have had a recent encounter with Corbett and Coryn."

"Even if I knew who you were talking about I would die before I turned them over to you."

"As you wish." She summoned her bow and arrow and readied it for Selene. Selene widen her eyes in fright and gripped Edel harder around his waist. Not like this, she thought. Out of nowhere sped an arrow into Esmereldas' neck.

"Arlis! Move!" called a voice.

Esmeralda looked up and pulled out the arrow. Selene watched her smile broadened as she galloped away with Edel after Arlis.

*   *   *

Luciana!" called Esmeralda in pure excitement.

"What?" said Luciana rather annoyed. She wanted some peace and quiet.

"I know what name Corbett goes by."

Luciana froze in happiness. She could hear her heart pounding in her ears.

"What name?"

"One you are all too familiar with. Arlis."

Luciana laughed. "Arlis. That is the alias I gave to him."

"I know, Trixie called him by that name."

"Trixie was there?"

Esmerelda nodded. "I was about to shoot the princess when she shot me in my neck and told Corbett to run."

"Brilliant. Send Nathaniel back to the tavern but this time tell him to keep hidden. Tell Adira to stop hunting for Donovan. They will be coming to me and we will meet than in that disgusting hovel of tavern. In the meantime, kill everyone in the village. Spare no one."

Esmerelda bowed. "Of course milady."

Luciana propped herself on her window ledge and smiled; she paid Nora no heed when she came from the shadows.

"Are you pleased?"

"Beyond pleased. How stupid is he to use that name. Does he want me to find him? Does she think all of this is some sort of game?"

"Apparently so."

"This is all so amusing. Get the twins up here Nora, I would like to have a word with them."

Nora bowed and went out of the room, this time using the door. Finally Corbett had been found, and with the princess, thought Luciana as she dug her nails into the marble.

*   *   *

Without hardly stopping they rode. Selene was ready to collapse and looked at Edel who looked tired as well. For nights they had trotted along, sneaking into naps here and there. Whoever had saved them, those many days ago, knew Arlis. That must have been her. Selene looked over at Arlis who also looked tired. He seemed to be looking for something.

"Halt!" came a voice.

Selene looked around frightened. Arlis got off his horse and took a step forward. And arrow shot in front of him

"I said halt!"

"Cade, put down your arrow! Now!"

Selene watched as a girl stepped forward from behind the thick trees. Selenes' eyes widened in happiness and relief when she recognized the face. It was someone she had met on her way to Isabelles' Tavern.

"Nila!"

"Hello princess. Nice to see you again."

Selene smiled and then a thought crossed her mind. "You know Arlis?"

Nila nodded. "He wanted me to keep an eye on you when you fled. He was very protective of you."

"Still am," muttered Arlis.

Selene watched a bemused smiled cross Nilas face when she looked at Arlis through the corner of her eye. Selene ignored it, whatever secrets they had were their own.

"So you are the one we are here to meet?"

She nodded. "Among others." She tilted her head sideways and smiled. "And how are you Edel?"

"I'm fine. Arlis why didn't you ever tell us it was Nila we were meeting?"

"I wanted it to be a pleasant surprise."

Nila laughed. "Well come here, Arlis. Now who are your friends."

"You already know Edel, Selene and Blake. The rest are Artemisa, Dorian, Neva, Iris, Sage, Lief, Castor, Nyx, Nerox, Silvia, Crystal, Aidan and Rose." Each nodded a hello toward Nila who looked different, older, wiser.

"Hello."

"Wait," started Selene, "you know Nila Blake?"

"Of course. Remember, I met Arlis in the village and we were fast friends. Then when you came to the village he sent mt to go find Nila."

"Oh," said Selene. What was with her she thought, why was she questioning her friends, she should trust them. *Betrayers* . . . Selene shook her head, and looked around; where had that whisper come from.

"Well don't just sit there, follow me, I have a small camp already set up."

They all followed Nila on their horses that were worn and exhausted just like their masters and stopped at a camp. There were elves everywhere, staring at them all in hot curiosity.

"Everyone," began Nila, "this is my friend Arlis, he was the one we were waiting for." She turned to Arlis. "Arlis these are my friends. Cade, Henry, Calpurnia, Tifone, Alexander, Muir, Sadira, Belinda, Timiony, Lennox, Sandie, Golfiend, Eorfearst, Rivceian, and Taereis."

"I'm sorry for firing at you, had I know who you were I would have not tried to be so hostile," said Cade timidly.

"It's all right, don't worry about it," said Arlis.

"Nila were they ones who fired at the General?" asked Selene.
Yes."

"How long have you been watching us?"

"Since I saw you in the town."

"Oh."

A bit of sadness overwhelmed Nila. "Yes General Esmerelda is most arrogant, even for an elf."

"How do you know?"

"We elves know a lot about her. She was supposed to be the future queen. She joined to stop the dark lord, her and her sister, but she was killed and turned into *her* service. They say that her sister died of heart break, leaving her husband and daughter alone."

Betrayers . . ."Why do you know so much?"

"Because I was alive, a child, but alive none the less. Most of us were present at the funeral."

"How old are you?"

"I would rather not say if you don't mind? She smiled and poked at the fire. "So, Arlis, how are you?"

"You've already asked that, when are we going to meet your cousin?"

"Soon."

"You have a cousin?" asked Selene.

"His name is Galen. He's on the run at the moment. After sabotaging some of General Adira's work he has a pretty high price on his head."

"Oh."

"Yeah, being a rebel can get quite exciting." She laughed and sat back on a rock.

"Blake, I don't think I've asked how you are?"

"I'm all right, thank you. Are you sure it's safe to stay here?"

"For tonight. Knowing the *queen* she probably will have all her generals looking for you princess now that they've seen you."

"You act as thought you know her," stated Selene. Corbett glared at Trixie who retained her composer.

"I've studied her. Since her rise to power. It's best to try and know your opponent, especially in action. It's how you win a war princess."

"Nila could you please stop calling me princess, my name Selene, leave it at that."

"As you wish." She smiled and went back to tending the fire. Selene looked over to where Edel sat with Blake and Arils. She stood up and watched him follow her into the dark forest.

"We shouldn't be out here. We should stay close to them."

"Edel why is this happening?"

"Because some fool obviously made a grave mistake. He rejected a love offered to him, scorned her for a princess, your ancestor, the general Norà. Foolishness caused all of this."

"It's not fair Edel, it's simply isn't." She went over to him and buried herself in his chest.

"Don't worry Selene, we're going to make her pay for all the pain she has caused." Selene looked up at Edel and kissed him fiercely, wrapping her arms around his neck. She felt him wrap his arms around tightly around her waist and kiss her back. Suddenly, to Selenes shock, he pushed her away and smiled his crocked smile, his dimple's making her love him far more.

"Edel—"

"Shh, come on let's get back to the fire, it's safe there, and besides, you need your rest." Selene nodded in agreement and let herself be dragged back to the fire.

*　　*　　*

"You almost slipped up," hissed Corbett, not wanting to wake anyone up.

"I fixed my mistake didn't I, no damage was done," said Trixie.

"Enough you two, we can't use this conflict, we need to make sure that we stay strong," said Coryn.

"You're not our king, not a prince anymore Coryn, so stop talking as thought you are," snapped Corbett.

"Hey don't take out your anger on him," began Trixie, "it's not his fault you screwed up and . . ." Trixie stopped and covered her mouth in shock.

"And what? Cursed us all, cursed all those that I loved? Come on say it!"

"Enough. Trixie can you just tell us the real story with Donovan and Adira."

"He sabotaged an attack of hers on a village and now she's tracking him. But I have a feeling that Luciana is going to recall all her troops back the to Onyx Fortress, now that enough has been discovered."

"Hmm, so he'll be meeting us soon," said Corbett. He had quickly calmed himself despite himself, after all Coryn was right and he knew that.

"There is a village nearby. His men are there, hiding out, protecting the people secretly. From there we should cut through the forest, it'll save us on time, especially is we ride hard some days."

"How much time."

"A months, maybe two. My elves will run in the trees, they're faster in the tree tops."

"At least they can keep a heads up, keep watch," said Corbett.

"Exactly what I was thinking," said Trixie. She took out an arrow and played with the feathered end. "We don't have much of an army."

"We'll win."

"Our immortality is fading."

"So is theirs, which means they can die as well."

"She out numbers us."

"We will win."

"I hope we don't lose many, we've already lost so much." A tear ran down her cheek and Corbett knelt down and hugged her. "I miss my sister Corbett."

"I know, shh."

"Corbett, she's right, we can't afford to lose more people we love."

"I know," he said more hostile. He knew what was at stake, he knew far more that anyone did.

Corbett left Trixie in the arms of Coryn and walked for a while till he reached the edge of the river. He remembered it all . . .

Luciana and Corbett were the sneaky ones, getting a head start and checking out their enemy. They snuck around boulders on the barren land, and stopped at the lake of darkness.

"Corbett, how in the world are we supposed to get in? That army is far to vast."

"We'll get through, trust me, I have a plan." He smiled his best smile, but Luciana, for once, did not smile back.

"Corbett, we are about to enter battle, we could die."

"Stop thinking like that Luciana," he cupped her face in his hands dirt covered hands and stared at her.

"Corbett—" He kissed her. It felt so right and he wondered how he had never realized it. How could I be so stupid, he asked himself.

Luciana pulled her face away and stared at him, longingly.

"Reliving fond memories' Corbett," said a cold voice. Corbett opened his eyes and before him stood Luciana, green eyed and hurt.

"Luciana." He drew out his sword and pointed the blade towards her. Luciana stood her ground and he knew he could do it, and that he wanted to do it, and that he should do it, but he couldn't. All he wanted to do was hold her in his arms once again and kiss her lovingly again.

"Even if you dared, it wouldn't do any good Corbett," she hissed. She crossed her arms and Corbett threw down his sword.

"What do you want Luciana?"

"Just wanted to see you, is that so bad?" Her mockery was plain to see. Corbett walked to her and noted the warm smile that crossed her face. This isn't your Luciana, he told himself over rand over again, as he longed to hold her, to kiss her.

"You're not my Lucania," he finally forced himself to say. He watched as her face became dark and as her eyes and nails turned black in colour.

"And you're not my Corbett, but you don't see me complaining."

"That's because you have nothing to complain about. You're the queen, rule of all Radiencia. You have nothing to complain about," he smiled at her and her eyes turned back to their beautiful emerald jade colour. Corbett also softened and stroked her face.

"I hate you Corbett."

"I know."

"You left me to die."

"I know."

"I hate you."

"Then come away with me. Lets just runaway and forget all of this, leave it all behind."

"You scorned me!" Her eyes turned pitch black and her hatred flared all around.

"You betrayed us!"

"Who betrayed who first Corbett? You left me to die!"

He stared at her hatefully. "I should have killed you when I had the chance."

Luciana smiled malevolently. "Yes you should have." She paused and stared at him thoughtfully. "I how you have an army Corbett, or our battle will be a pathetic one."

"I will kill you."

Luciana laughed as she turned on her heel.

"No, you won't . . . you can't." Her laughter echoed off the trees as she vanished.

Chapter Seven

Corbett stood amongst the group, and examined them throughly. This wasn't really an army., in fact it wasn't one at all, it was just a group of friends that had joined together to fight. Trixie pulled him aside. He hadn't told and of them that Luciana had come, but it would be common knowledge for her, especially with her elfin hearing.

"You are an idiot!" she scolded.

"It was nothing," he growled back.

"I don't care about *her*. Cade heard every word, saw everything. I had to tell him everything!" She paused and looked at him. "He doesn't hate her as he once did Corbett, in fact he pities her. We betrayed her first, and all this," she waved her hands about her, "all this is our doing, not hers."

"That's does not excuse what she has done."

"No, but it does excuses what she has become." She began to walked away but stopped and tilted her head back towards him. "You should have kissed her when you asked her to run away with you, it would have ended everything, stopped all of this at once."

"Just leave Trixie," he said through clenched teeth.

"We all broke her heart Corbett, not just you." She left and Corbett pulled out his sword and began striking a tree trunk with uncontrollable rage. Damn her, he thought as he fell to the ground in tears.

*   *   *

Selene sat on her horse half asleep. She had not gotten any sleep for the past few nights. Faces were blurred and the dream had been cold, but familiar voices warmed the cold forlorn set of the dream. She had heard Nila and Arlis and Luciana. It was her face and only her face that had been plain to see. There were others as well who had stood around, their voices inaudible. Isabelle had stood her face also clear and filled with anger and remorse. People stood around, the generals had appeared, their faces plain and filled with malevolence. Others surrounded the palace of the forlorn land. Vehement shown in Lucianas' as she pulled her sword and threw it in front of the feet of the man standing next to Selene. His voice, she knew, she knew him, if only she could place him.

Selene could feel herself slipping from her saddle and she knew she would have fallen if not a hand had steadied her.

"Selene," asked Edel, "are you all right?"

"No," she answered bluntly. "I've been having these horrible dreams. There are blurry faces but distinct voices. I can't remembered much accept darkness. But I remember hearing and seeing Luciana and Isabelle and the voices of Arlis and Nila." They all looked at each other and then back towards Selene.

"She's placed a curse on you," said Nila. Her eyes narrowed. "Have you been near something dark?"

"A dark petal found it's way onto my pillow."

"Great, she found a way into your mind," said Nila sarcastically. She swore under her breath and bit on her thumb.

"But I was able to get off the bed before anything occurred, before it spread."

"Doesn't matter; even if you burned the sheets, so close your mouth Arlis." Selene looked at Arlis who had usually hardened expression contorted in anger and frustration. Selene finally remembered. The petal had fallen on her forehead first.

"So what do I do?"

"I don't know, we'll have to try a spell or potion. Cade, go find some herbs, any that you know have magical properties and bring them back quickly." She turned to Arlis. "Keep an eye on her, and you," she said turned to Selene, "get some sleep." With that, Nila ran into the forest after Cade.

"Come here Selene," said Edel getting off his horse. Selene nodded and got off the horse, falling into Edel's arms.

"Edel . . . the petal landed on my forehead before it landed on the bed." Edel looked down at her, a frightened look in his eyes.

"Selene—"

"Don't tell anyone, please."

"I have to tell . . . it's for your own good."

"No!" she screamed. Everyone looked at her and Corbett stared at her. That was not Selene's voice.

Luciana was angry. Who was this person to foul up her plans. She needed Trixie to make the potion, to fall into her trap.

"Selene," said Edel. "Trust me."

"No!" screamed Luciana. She swore, why did that stupid girl have to mention it fell on her.

"Screaming won't help Luciana," said Nora.

Luciana glared at her. "Shut up."

"Don't get mad at us," said Adira.

"I didn't want to deal with plan B, but I guess I don't have a choice do I." She looked at her generals who all shook their heads. Luciana walked away from her mirror and grabbed two swords.

"Lets go give my sister a visit then. I'll need her to prove all that I need." She walked out of her home and got on her horse, followed by her Generals.

Selene shook her head and looked up at Edel. He stared down at her worried.

"Are you all right?"

"Yeah, sure, I'm sorry, I don't know what came over me. We should tell." A tear escaped down her cheek. "Edel what's happening?" She buried her head in her chest and cried.

"Shh, it's all right, don't worry."

Corbett looked at Coryn. Luciana was up to something, and she was on their tail.

"Come on Selene," said Edel, "you must get some sleep." Selene nodded and slunk down next to a tree, her eyes fluttering closed. Sleep, yes, that what I need, she thought to herself.

*   *   *

Luciana rode, quickly. She didn't have time for this. She didn't want to deal with her sister, it would take to much out of her, to much magic, too much emotion.

"Luci—" began Damian.

"You are not to call me that!"

"Ignore him Luciana, but I think what he was going to say was, we will deal with this on our own, you've no need to come," said Nora.

"No. I'll do the first half, I need to, but you will perform the second." She drew her horse to a halt and got down gracefully. She took off her armour, and the others followed suit, quietly and carefully, they were in no rush.

Luciana unlocked the door with a simple touch and crept inside, silencing any creaks. The tavern was empty and Luciana saw an old happy memory. They were all laughing again, drunk and being idiots. Luciana didn't smile at the joyful memory, instead her face hardened and her nails sunk into her skin.

The place grew cold and Luciana opened her sisters bedroom door. She walked in, her head held high, and a evil smile creeping on her face.

Luciana stepped onto the bed softly so as not to wake her dearly beloved sister. She stood over her and watched as Nora and Nathaniel stood on either side of her, ready to grab her and hold her down. Luciana bent down to her sisters ear.

"Time to wake up little sister dear."

Isabelle jerked her eyes open and gasped.

"Luciana—"

"Hello Isabelle, how are you? Question why don't you perform some magic?"

"Get out of here."

"A single spell Bella, just a simple spell will make me go away."

Isabelle gritted her teeth. "I can't perform magic."

"Of course you can, I *know* you can. So let's see what you have done shall we." Luciana grabbed her sisters' face and sunk her nail into her eyes. They would heal but she needed to see, and her sisters' cries of pain filled Luciana with joy. Nora and Nathaniel held her down easily as she tried to get out of their grasps. Luciana saw their childhood, their lives, everything from her birth to this point. Finally her anger flared. She took her nails out of her slapped her hard, cutting deep into her skin.

"You selfish brat!" Damien grabbed her around the waist and pulled her down. He had his dagger at his waist and Luciana grabbed it and put it to her sisters' throat.

"I should kill you know for what you have done, but that would be merciful. Watch, I will kill all that you love and put you in my cell where I suffered! I will make you pay Isabelle, and I will let them know of your treachery."

"They will never believe you."

"No, but they will believe your precious princess now won't they." Luciana gave Damien back his dagger, slamming it hard against his chest as she turned to leave. An arrow went through her forehead; Luciana smiled and pulled it out of her head. She turned back to her sister, her wound already healed.

"Watch your arrow." Luciana grasped it and it turned to ash. "You're so pathetic." She turned to Nora and the rest. "Finish."

Isabelle jerked up from bed, a layer of cold sweat on her body. It was just a nightmare. She wiped her face and looked at the dried blood on her hand. She must have cut herself again, she thought. Isabelle got up and walked to her mirror, her past still haunted her and always would. Thunder struck and in that flash, Isabelle swore she saw her sister on her window sill in her dark armour, but when she turned around, no one was there. She went back to bed and fell straight asleep.

"I'm sorry Luci."

"Not good enough."

Isabelle jerked up again, and looked around. She was alone as she always was.

Luciana sat on a branch outside her sisters' window with Nathaniel.

"So it's true then?"

Luciana nodded. "A piece of me had hope against it."

"I held that same hope."

Luciana smiled. "We are too human you and I."

"Our hearts were already damaged." He let out a sigh. "I never did thank you did I."

"For what?"

"Saving me."

"You don't have to."

"Yes I do. If it were not for you, I would be dead."

"Hmm." Nathaniel spun her around and kissed her. Luciana kissed him back and then pushed him away.

"We are far to alike." She smiled and felt her eyes shift.

"Your eyes Luci."

"Never mind them, come, we have a battle to prepare for." She jumped down and walked to her horse. He had called her Luci and for once, she hadn't minded.

*　*　*

In the dead of night Corbett wandered away from the crowd. He wanted to see Luciana again but he knew his hopes would be in vain. She hated him, like he hated her but he missed her nonetheless.

Finally in a nice secluded place, far away from the camp, Corbett laid down. He stared up at the moon, a pang of guilt struck him. It was all his fault.

It was because of him Luciana and his friends were cursed; it was because of him that Selene was suffering. Everything was his fault.

"Not entirely."

Corbett sat up, next to him was Luciana, his Luciana. She smiled at him and he couldn't help himself. He sat up and kissed her.

"Come away with me Luci."

"Never." She pulled away and looked at him. "I can never forgive you, any of you."

He sighed and layed back down. "Leave the princess alone, she has suffered enough." He felt Luciana lay on his chest and he wrapped his arm around her, holding her close.

"Maybe."

"Why don't you just kill us now?"

"Now where would the fun be in that?" She laughed and sat up.

"You disgust me." She stopped laughing and stared down at him.

"I will make her suffer Corbett. You have seen nothing yet." She disappeared and Corbett sat up and looked at the little pool of water.

Luciana was splashing around and he jumped in, tackling her. She screamed in delight.

"Corbett come on." He was tickling her and she couldn't help but jerk and laugh. He just wanted to be alone with her, he loved her. He stopped tickling her and kissed her again.

"Luci—"

"Yes?"

"When this is all over . . . Will you marry me?" Luciana kissed him lovingly then pulled away and smiled.

"Of course Corbett."

Corbett opened his eyes. What did he do? He got up and walked into the little pool. He needed to forget all those memories. His Luci was long gone.

Chapter Eight

Luciana was practising her archery. She hit the bullseye time and time again. She kept imagining that it was her sisters head. Someone wrapped their arms around her waist and kissed her neck.

"Hello Nathaniel."

"You visited Corbett."

"It was a mistake," she growled. She shot another arrow, this time pretending it was Corbetts head. "'Nice shot."

"Thank you." She dropped her arrow and bow and spun around. It had been six centuries since anyone had kissed her this tenderly.

"Enough already," came Nora's voice.

"Go away Nora."

"No. Nathaniel leave us, I need to talk to her majesty."

"Of course," he smiled and walked out.

"What Nora?"

"You cannot be doing this."

"I need an heir anyway, might as well be him." Luciana picked up her arrow and began practising again.

"I thought the plan was to trick Corbett."

"It still is."

"You visited him correct?"

"Part of the plan."

"One question then: is it working?"

"Seems to be, especially when my eye are green; I'm his Luci whenever that happens."

"You seem to be Nathaniels' as well, no matter what colour your eyes are."

"Shut up."

"I see the attraction though," continued Nora ignoring her. "Isabelle shoot him when he yelled for her help and you saved him. He feels the betrayal like you do." Nora let down her hair and leaned against the wall. "Will you be able to kill him when the time comes?"

"Yes." She shot an arrow next to Nora's next; she smiled.

"Nice shot."

"What are you talking about, I missed." Luciana dropped her stuff. "I'm going to bed."

"Have fun Luciana."

Luciana laughed. "I hope to." She walked away and down the hallway to her bedroom. There, sitting on her bed was Nathaniel.

"Hello Luci."

She smiled and kissed him. "How's my favourite general?"

"I'm fine, now enough talk." He kissed her back tenderly and laid her on the bed. Who needs Corbett, she thought.

*   *   *

Selene finally got some sleep, for two days straight. It was most welcomed. They were taking a break to eat and practice their skills. She just sat there and ate while she watched Edel practice his swordsmanship with Artemisa; he had a natural talent; unfortunately, for him Artemisa disarmed him, tripped him and won. Edel just laughed. Artemisa was very talented. Artemisa helped him up and he dusted himself off.

"Your turn Selene," said Artemisa.

"Uh, all right, I might as well." Edel handed her his swords and she got the feel of it. Soon they began to spar. Selene was very talented and the swords felt right in her hand.

Selene wouldn't give until Artemisa was down. Suddenly a scene flashed in front of her eyes. Luciana was laughing, with green eyes and her white robe. Sparing with her was Nora, dressed like Selene was. Selene swung harder, she would not end up like Nora.

"Selene, I give already," cried Artemisa. Selene realized the scene. Her sword was against Artemisa's inching it's way toward her face as she was against a tree.

"Oh my god, Artemisa, I'm so sorry."

"Yeah okay—" She snatched the sword from her and looked at her. "What the hell is wrong with you?!"

"I . . . I don't know. Oh my god, I'm so sorry."

"Artemisa she's sorry okay relax, she had no idea of what she was doing," said Edel taking back his sword.

"Selene sit down," said Nila soothingly. Selene did so. "What did you see?" she asked in hushed whisper.

"Luciana and Nora were laughing sparing." She rubbed her face. "Nila, what's going on?"

"I don't know sweety, really. It sounds as though she's giving you her memories. I may need to make another potion or something, I'm not even sure." Nila rubbed her back to try sooth her. "Don't worry, this will all be over soon. I promise."

"Nila?"

"Yes?"

"Esmeralda, she was to be the elf queen, correct?"

"Yes, but, she was taken and her sister soon after giving birth died of heart break."

"Do you talk of it? Of what she has become?"

"No, no one does. It's not a very fond memory."

"Memory?"

"Of the people, none of us wish to remember it"

"That's right, you're elves, you live long."

Nila smiled at her. "Get to sleep Selene, I know it may not be pleasant, and you may see more of her memories, but you need sleep. I'll be back with more herbs soon."

Selene nodded. Sleep was what she needed. Unfortunately it was not what she got.

Selene was back behind the tapestry once again, with Edel holding her quiet. Her face was clouded in darkness. Selene was suddenly pulled from behind the tapestry.

Luciana was gripping her, an evil sneer plastered on her face.

"This isn't a dream," whimpered Selene.

"Oh no princess, this is me invading your mind." Luciana thrust her against the wall. Two figures appeared next to her. They were generals Nora and Nathaniel.

"Get out of my head!" ·

"I don't think so." She looked around. "So this is how you escaped. Who's that behind the tapestry, your servant boy." She went to lift the tapestry.

"You leave Edel alone."

Lucian looked at her and smiled. "Edel? Oh I don't care about you precious 'Edel', it's Corbett I want."

"I don't know Corbett!"

"So you think." Luciana looked Selene up and down through scrutinizing eyes. "You perform magic correct, so you know the power of a name."

"Yes, I know, what do you want."

"Nothing, I just wanted to know what makes you so appealing to Corbett. All I see is something he lost, a long time ago."

She snapped her fingers and Selene opened her eyes. It was dusk, she had slept the day away.

"Hey finally you're awake," said Edel. Selene looked at him and smiled, no one had to know what she dreamt.

"Yup." She stretched. "That was needed honesty, and truly needed."

"That's good, that you finally got some sleep." He pulled her up. "Nila has another potion for you to drink but be warned, it smells quite foul." He laughed.

"Joy." They walked to Nila who looked up and gave her a weak smile.

"I can do nothing for the smell, the only advice I have is, don't think about it, just swallow it down, quickly." She grabbed a cup from her pack and poured the foul liquid into it. Selene slowly lifted the cup to her face and drank it down as quick as she could and tried with all her might not to vomit.

"I think I'm going to be sick," she said dropping the cup. She felt Edel steady her as she slipped to the ground.

"Are you all right?"

"That was vile." Edel laughed and she smiled. Hopefully this would work.

*   *   *

Corbett stood aside with Trixie and Coryn; he had watched Selene as she practised, and it was not Selene he had seen. It was Nora. Why had he kissed Nora in the first place. He knew that he loved Luciana, and he had planned to go back for her. He was still asking himself, still trying to figure out why he had not gone back for her, trying to figure out what had made him go to that lake, trying to figure out what made him kiss Nora.

When she took a rest, he had watched as her breathing became heavier. Something had happened, her dream was not a dream

"Trixie, what are we going to do?"

"I don't know, the potions don't seem to be helping much do they." She bit down on her nail nervously. "Corbett, Luciana is up to something."

"Of course she is, she always is, we all know that."

"I know but I mean, something other than that. I don't like how all this feels."

Coryn coughed and they looked at him. "What? That stuff smells foul." Corbett couldn't help but smile. It had been a while since he smiled. Trixie threw a branch at his head and he looked at her startled.

"What was that for?"

"I see the way you look at the princess. Stop it, mean it."

"Those are my personal—"

"Shut up. Look, I was waiting till we had everyone together but you need to hear this now. You can't kill Luciana, none of us can, we can only destroy the outside, the shell, her body. She killed his body, but his essence went to her. He needed someone broken, angry, and powerful. That was Luciana. Corbett, Selene is powerful:, and I fear that if by any chance you succeeded in killing her, that Luciana has a plan. Selene, that is what I sense. I'm worried about her as well as you, I don't think you couldn't handle that again."

He ignored the comments about himself and stared at her. "She'll be fine, there isn't anything that Luciana can do."

He looked at Trixie who looked unconvinced and unsure. "I hope you're right . . . for all our sakes, especially yours."

"You are being far to over dramatic."

Trixie looked at him with an impossible expression on her face and punched him, knocking him back into the tree behind him. Corbett stood stunned and held his jaw, shocked.

"And you aren't taking this seriously at all. This all our last chance to stop her Corbett, if we fail, we are all damned. We have to destroy this darkness Corbett, before it spreads even more." With that, she stalked off. Coryn looked back and forth not knowing what to do. Finally he walked over to Corbett.

"Uh— "

"I'm fine," he growled.

"Good, good. Well we should probably—"

"You go back, I . . . look I need some air okay."

Coryn nodded and walked away leaving Corbett alone. He needed some time alone as well and sat by a tree. Trixie was right; they weren't taking it that seriously. They were only adamant on killing Luciana, and that by itself, was doomed to fail. He unsheathed his sword and began to spar with himself.

He needed to get better if he even wanted a chance of defeating his once beloved sister.

"Careful brother, you might hurt yourself." Coryn stopped and slowly turned around. Standing right in front of him was his sister, her bright blue eyes cloaked in poison.

"Nora," he said hushed. She smiled and pulled out her sword. As she walked over to him, she danced her techniques, belittling him.

"You know I was always the better swordsman. If that old fool of man had just let me practice, I could have been great, but no, I was the princess, subjected to magic. Never did have the patience for it."

Coryn smiled. "You harbor far too much hatred and jealously sister."

"I was first born! I should have been trained for the throne, not you!"

Coryn's smile broadened. "Jealously doesn't suit you sister; it always did make you ugly."

Nora lunged at him, but he blocked her, nearly stumbling over a lifted tree root. Nora regained herself composure and smiled at him.

"Let's duel little brother."

"I am not your brother, and you are not my sister." He lunged and they spared for a bit, but Coryn was growing sick. His royal symbol, made him queasy, but this time, more than ever.

"What's wrong little brother, feeling sick?" She knocked his sword out of his hand and walked toward him, making him stumble back onto the ground.

"You always were a pathetic fighter." She sneered and turned around. "I'll have your head, and you can count on that." Then she was gone in a surge of black mist.

Coryn sat there for a few minutes more before he finally forced himself up and dusted himself off. He grabbed his sword and examined it throughly. There on the hilt was the pure royal symbol, his symbol. He couldn't really blame Nora for being what she is now, she had always resented him, but she had loved him, all the same and had always made time to help him perfect his swordsmanship and with unyielding patience which his tutors lacked. But Luciana took away the love and patience and left only the resentment and hatred. He sighed, his sister was gone.

Chapter Nine

Nora practised her swordsmanship with Damien. He didn't look like a half elf, but he was one nonetheless. He practised against her sword with his black dagger. Nora was angry, but she always used her anger for the better. Her little brother had gotten the better of her.

"Relax Nora," soothes Damien as he batted of her sword, again.

"The throne should have been mine."

"Now it belongs to no one, doesn't that make you happy?" He saw a smile creep onto her face.

"Very." She thrust her sword in his daggers, knocking them out of his hold. An old family move that the tutors failed to teach Coryn, something she also failed to teach him, treasuring her unsurpassed ability.

"I'm lucky only you can perform that."

"Yes you are." She sheathed her sword and sharpened her nails quickly against the wall. She smiled delightfully when Lucas and Jason walked into the room. And looked around blankly.

"What do you two want," said Nora. They looked at her and smiled.

"We need to see Luciana," they said.

"She's in bed with Nathaniel, why."

"She's in bed with Nathaniel, finally," said Lucas.

"He's been ranting about her since she took the throne seven years ago," said Jason.

"Get on with it," said Nora rather irritated.

"Oh well, we need to talk to her about the plan she commissioned for us."

"Which being?"

"Poison the elfin lands." They snickered.

"How did you manage that?" asked Damien amused.

"We posed, well I posed as a farmer," said Lucas.

"And I posed as a smith, not that hard really. Everything they eat—"

"Poison," finished Lucas.

"And everything they touch—"

"Poison." They laughed again.

"Is the plan succeeding then," asked Nora.

"Going smoothly, some are even taking up the dark arts."

"Quite fanciful really, she'll love it."

"Yes she will. I'll call her, hopefully she'll take out her wrath on some poor peasant." They all laughed and Nora quickly silenced them all. "Luciana."

Luciana heard the call but she was to busy in the arms and kisses of Nathaniel. She didn't have to been to be seen, she concluded.

"What?" Luciana's word bounced off the wall. She couldn't help but moan in delight and Nora couldn't help but smile.

"Are we disturbing you?"

"Get on with it!" Nathaniels fingers traced up her leg.

"Lucas and Jason wanted to update you on their progress. All is well, figuratively speaking and the elves are slowly dying or turning toward darkness."

"Good, now go do something constructive that does not involve me!" She ended her spell and encircled Nathaniels neck as she kissed him fiercely.

"So how is my queen?" he muttered in her ear.

"Very pleased" she breathed.

*   *   *

Corbett didn't know why his heart ached. It just did. It wasn't the guilt, he knew how that felt, and it wasn't anger, he knew how that felt as well, what he couldn't figure out was why it felt like it was breaking into two, like he was losing someone he cared about. He looked around. It had been two days since their last rest. He still couldn't figure out why Nora had come to see her brother. That worried him. Luciana he understood why she would make a visit, but why Nora. Suddenly he began to worry about the others. He could deal with visitations but he didn't think that the others could. Coryn could have been killed and if Esmerelda visited her little sister, Trixie would surely fall beneath her feet. Isabelle, it wasn't Luciana he worried about, but rather

Nathaniel; Isabelle wouldn't admit it but she loved him still. And then there was Donovan. He loved to toy around with Adira, the question was how much.

Corbett often worried that his two best friends, Lucas and Jason would come, to that Damien would come and tantalize Trixie, again. She had loved him, and he her, but since she was a princess, it was never meant to be, especially since he was no better than a half elf of lower nobility.

"What are you thinking about," asked Trixie as they trotted along.

"Why did she visited Coryn. I still don't get it."

"Stop fussing over it, it won't help. Look . . . I know you're worried about us. Coryn is still shaken up by the whole thing. He misses her."

"You can shoot your sister from afar, but what about if she comes to you, like Nora with Coryn?" He looked at Trixie hard who looked frightened.

"I—I d-don't know," she stuttered.

"Well you had better find our because in battle I know for a fact that Luci will pit—" He stopped talking. What the hell, he thought.

"Corbett, did you just call her Luci?"

"Enough, lets just keep going but as I was saying, I know Luciana will sent our loved ones after us. Esmerelda after you, Nora after Coryn, Adira after Donovan, even perhaps Entia after him, Nathaniel after Isabelle and she'll come after me herself. I think she'll even send Lucas and Jason after me and Damien after you. It's how Luciana thinks."

"And of course you are the expert on Luciana." she said hotly.

"Don't take that tone Trixie, not with me."

"And why not?" She pulled her horse in front of him and looked back at the princess nervously. She was asleep.

"Before you talk about us and how we'll react, think about yourself, Corbett, she is the one that has to be stopped, and you're the one that has to stop her. Do not think that you are superior to us Corbett, because you are far from it." She trotted ahead and from the corner of his eye he saw a horse appear next to him.

"She's right you know," said Cade.

"This is far beyond you," hissed Corbett.

"No it's not. You love Luciana and she loves you. All you have to do—"

Luciana screamed, and it echoed across the land. The sky darkened and the wind sped faster. There was muttering across the sky and Corbett recognized the makings of a spell.

Selene woke up startled and pulled out her sword she knew she would need it.

"Edel, what's happening?" He shook his head and pulled out his sword.
"I don't know."

Coryn looked around. He knew what was about to happen.

"Prepare yourselves!" he yelled over the brewing storm.

Corbett jumped off his horse and looked around.

Luciana got dressed and walked to her mirror.

"Show him to me!" she screeched. She saw him preparing for battle. A malevolent smile crossed her face as she snapped her fingers.

The dead rose all around them, and Corbett destroyed one quickly. He saw this coming, he knew this was going to happen.

Luciana placed herself behind a tree. The dead were everywhere, people die everywhere and right now, she wanted the elf to die.

"Kill him," she breathed.

Corbett heard her and looked over at Cade. He needed to get to him. Luckily Trixie was faster. Trixie batted away another un-dead. She had heard Luciana order his death and she would not allow it.

Corbett looked around and stopped. Luciana was standing there, beyond the fight. He could kill her, he could get to her.

"Turn around Corbett," she said as she vanished. Corbett did and saw Damien ready an arrow and aim it not at Cade but Trixie.

"No!" He tried to lunged but a cold hand stopped him and spun him to the ground. His sword was flung from his hand and Luciana lay next to him, holding him down.

"You will lose Corbett."

"What do you want?"

"For you to suffer!"

Someone screamed and Corbett knew that it was Trixie. Luciana was gone and so was Damien. Corbett grabbed his sword and ran toward Cade and Trixie. Coryn reached her first and Corbett chopped the head of another un-dead minion. Finally it all stopped and everything once alive was dead again.

"Nila," yelled Selene.

Corbett laid his weapon down and laid by her side. The arrow went right through her shoulder and attache her to an uprooted root. She was going to have to pull her.

"Scream okay, it's all right." Trixie nodded and Corbett grabbed her tightly. "Just breath," He pulled her forward and her scream shook the world. He knew her plan, she wanted to expose them for the frauds they were. Cade and Coryn tightly bound the wound that would heal quickly.

"Don't worry Selene, she'll be all right." He smiled after pulling her up. Trixie sheathed her sword and tried not to move her arm. She noticed that the bleeding wasn't stopping, and that her wound was taking a while to heal.

Damien stood behind a tree, far enough not to be seen, but close enough to see. A satisfied smile crossed his face. He felt someone appear next to him. He turned his head and there stood Esmerelda.

"Nice shot." She stood still, staring straight ahead.

"Why thank you, it come from centuries of practice," a sardonic smile crossed his face. Finally a smile came upon her face.

"You put poison on the tip didn't you."

"Luciana's orders."

"She is suck a sneaky devil," Esmerelda laughed. "To busy hiding their secret, they didn't notice the quickly growing infection. They fell right into her trap.

"Good thinking too, it was all last minute I honestly didn't think it would work."

"You should never doubt her Damien, she is Luciana after all."

"True. Come, we should probably get back to her majesty." They both smiled and disappeared.

Trixie looked up from the gathering crowd. She had seen Esmerelda's cold eyes and Damien's cocky sneer, something wasn't right, she could feel it.

*   *   *

Later that night, Corbett stood watch. Why did his heart ache, and why did he fell Luciana's dark magic very close. He looked around at everyone around him, and sopped at Trixie. Something was very wrong with her, something wasn't right. He kicked Coryn away and jerked awake, jumbling for his sword.

"Uh what? I'm ready," he said groggily.

"Shut up. Go check on Trixie, I'm worried about her."

"Oh okay." Coryn shook his head to wake himself and walked cat like towards Trixie. He touched her arm and pulled back quickly. Trixie was cold as ice.

"God. Corbett!"

"What?"

"She's cold." Corbett ran over to her body stealthily and rolled her over. She was still alive, her breathing was normal, but her body was cold and her lips were blue.

"Corbett what the hell is going on!" Coryn was never like this, never really angry, he was just always acting, but for once he wasn't and Corbett knew it.

"I don't know." Corbett quickly thought and the answer was right there in front of his face. He ordered Coryn to pull the arrow from the tree root and while he undressed her wound that should not be there. Blackness covered it.

Coryn returned and Corbett took the arrow from him and examined it.

"Corbett?"

"Trixie's been poisoned."

Chapter Ten

C orbett didn't know what to do. He had to play his part. He ordered Coryn to wake Cade and bring him over. When Cade arrived her grew sick to his stomach at just the sight of Trixie.

"What the hell am I supposed to do?"

"Pretend like you're the one that found her like this. This was a trap and we fell into it and I have a part to play that I can't reveal to Luciana. Just do it, quickly."

Corbett and Coryn flew to their sleeping positions and waited to wake till Cade shook them all.

*　　*　　*

Selene was the first to wake, in Edels arms. He jerked his eyes open as well. Cade was calling them all urgently.

"Cade, what's going on? When did you take over watch?"

"About an hour ago. It's Nila, I wanted to make sure that her wound was healing. She's been poisoned."

Murmurs arouse all around the camp. Selene saw the arrow on the ground and looked at the tree it once embedded. The bark was pitch black; it was dying.

"Oh god." She rushed to Nila's side and was taken aback but her touch; she was icy cold.

"How do we heal her? Arlis?" She looked up at him pleadingly and he knelt down to her.

"I don't know."

"What do you mean you don't know?!! Arlis do something!!"

"She needs some herbs, I know which type," said Blake suddenly. Selene looked at him questionably. "You do?"

He nodded. "Nila taught me a lot when I first met her. Cade come with me, we have to be quick."

"Understood."

They ran off and Selene hugged Nila to try to warm her.

"It won't help," said a voice.

"I can try Arlis! Dammit! How did they know we were here?!" Suddenly Selene knew. She took off her cloak and stood up. "Corbett show yourself! You're the reason this is happening to my friend! Stop being such a pathetic coward and show yourself!"

Corbett sat still. He could not expose himself, not while Luciana was in her mind.

"COWARD!!" Selene sat back down and stroked Nilas head. "Don't die Nila, please."

"Shh," soothed Edel, "she'll be fine, I know it."

"You can't be sure." Selene walked off and sat alone at a trunk of a tree, alone. She closed her eyes and was swept away to a dungeon. No one was around but she knew where to go. This was her home, or so she thought. These dungeons were colder than the ones at her palace, and she sensed pain, heard a faint scream, and cries. She walked out and up the cold stairs. The atmosphere changed and she sensed she was some place different, some place familiar. She looked down the stairs. It was different and she realized that this was her home. She had always hated it, it always frightened her, the darkness. She had to get out.

Finally to her relief she reached the door and entered a corridor. She knew which one too. She walked around feeling all the soft thick tapestries. They were all warm, cozy. To bad none of this was real she thought, she was alone, except for the faint click of her shoes upon the black marble floor.

Before long, she entered the throne room and the silver throne sat Luciana; everything once white was black and everything once gold, silver, drenched in darkness.

"Took you long enough," said Luciana casually examining her nails.

"They are looking for herbs, they'll save Nila."

"Nila?" Luciana laughed. Pathetic, she thought. She looked back the Princess, a slight smile on her face. "Too bad darling, they won't find any that will help her. Nila is doomed, but because I'm in a generous mood, I will give the antidote." Luciana waved vial daintily with her fingers. Selene stared at her frightened. She needed it whole, not spilt.

":What do you want?"

"Only the names of your companions."

"It isn't that simple."

"Ah but it is. Look darling Princess, this is the only antidote, I've poisoned the elven lands, and that's where I got this antidote, before the life turned dark." Luciana got off her throne and walked to her calmly. "Now, do you want the antidote or not?"

"Only the names right? You don't hurt them?"

"You have my word."

Your word means nothing to me, she thought, but she held her tongue. "Fine. Give me a pen and paper, I'll write them all down." Luciana smiled and snapped her fingers and a desk appeared, Selenes' fathers'. Tears welled up in her eyes but she had to do this, she had to help save Nila.

Luciana watched in satisfaction as Selene wrote down one name after another. Finally, when she was done, Luciana handed her the vial.

"How do I leave."

Luciana rolled her eyes and turned her back to her. "The same way anyone would, through the door."

Selene turned and ran and when she walked through the door, she woke up. The vial was cold in her hands and glowed a faint blue and for a minute she thought against what ever this was, but she knew she could trust the witch on this, even if her word meant nothing. As she walked back to camp, she began to think about how she would explain this to everyone. Honesty, that would be best.

Everyone was sitting around Nila, worry creases painted on all their faces. Selene gripped the vial and took a deep breath before walking into the midst of her friends.

"Selene," said Edel. His eyes drifted to the vial in her hands. "What's that?"

"The antidote for Nila."

"What?" exclaimed Arlis.

Selene kept her eyes cast down. "It's the antidote."

"Where did you get it," asked Corbett, but he already knew. Luciana.

"*She* came to me . . . again. She gave it to me—"

"In exchange for what?" asked Arlis.

"Your names." Corbett wanted to hit something, anything. What the hell was she playing at.

"Give Nila the antidote," said Cade. Selene did so and while she did, he glared at Corbett who found it hard to ignore him. This was all his fault.

Colour soon returned to Trixie face and she stopped shivering.

Corbett rubbed his hand over his face. Something needed to be said.

"Selene," said Edel.

"Yeah?"

"That was really good what you did."

"She's my friend, I had to. Besides, she only wanted names. Not much harm I guess." She feigned a smile. A lot of power was in a name. Edel smiled back and he kissed her on her forehead.

He grabbed her hand and pulled her away from all the people. Selene let herself be dragged away and she suddenly stopped. She just wanted to be alone with him.

"Edel?"

"Selene, there is something I have to say." Selene's eyes lit up. Suddenly Edel kissed her. He couldn't help it, and this time it was Selene who pulled away.

"I love you too Edel."

Luciana gasped in pain and fell to the ground clutching her heart. It felt like it was breaking.

"Luciana," came a voice. It was Damien. Tears welled up in her eyes as the pain was becoming unbearable. Damien help her up and held close as she sobbed. She felt something wrong with Corbett, like he himself was in pain. Their lives were almost as one.

"Damien—"

"Shh, Luci, shh. Don't worry, once we win the battle all this will be over."

"I h-hate him!"

"I know, come on, lets put you to bed." Luciana continued sobbing as he picked her up and carried her up the stairs to her bedchamber and there he laid with her stroking her beautiful face as she sobbed in his arms and fell asleep exhausted.

Damien could leave, he knew that probably the should, Nathaniel would be back soon, but he couldn't find the strength to pull away. He remembered when he first met her. She had saved him from getting caught. She had hid him away with her magic, as she herself has stolen something, and when all was done, she had looked down at him and held out her hand.

"My name is Luciana, but my friends call me Luci for short. You are?" He pushed himself up arrogantly and brushed her hand away. Rudely.

"Damien, and I didn't need your help."

Luciana scoffed. "Right; you would have been caught if it weren't for me."
"What are you anyway, a mage or a thief?"
"Both, equally." She turned around and he couldn't help but start after her.
"So why are you here?"

She turned to him. "Will you keep your voice down, or do you want to be caught? I needed this crystal," she said as she opened and closed her hand back up giving him a brief glance at the crystal. "Very powerful magic and it holds the key to the dark lords destruction."

Damien couldn't resist but laugh. "You're trying to bring Mr. Powerful down. Good luck."

"Won't need it," she said rather arrogantly. "The crystal helps increase the power of spells. My friends and I will stop him."

"Wow, a whole group of you. Do they know you're here?"

Luciana stopped short and looked at him. "No, Corbett would have wanted to do this, but I needed to."

"Why?"

She continued walking. "I just did. Why are you following me?"

"You saved me from being caught, I owe you one." He smiled down at her and she smiled back.

"All right . . . half-elf." She walked away and he stood stunned. "How did you—"

"Not that hard." She turned back to him. "I like half elves better than elves if it makes you feel better."

"Really?"

"Yes. Look I was just in the kingdom of the Elves and the princess' are nice, but the rest of them, obnoxious."

"Oh."

Suddenly she stopped walking in front of him, making him stumble. Once again she stuck out her hand.

"I'm Luciana."

"Damien," he said taking it.

He moved a strand of hair from her face and kissed her lightly on the lips. She was beautiful. She always had been and would always remain so. To bad for him that she had loved Corbett and that he had started to have feelings for Trixie and Trixie in return shared his feelings. He knelt down to her hear and kissed her neck.

"I always loved you." He kissed her again and he could feel her snuggle up on him. He smiled. So what if Nathaniel came back. He was only taking care of his friend.

"Damien— "

"Yes Luci?"

"I always liked you. I saved you because I had hoped that you would help me forget about *him*."

Damien smiled and kissed her head. "Go to sleep Luci." She nodded and went back to sleep.

"Get out," hissed a voice. Damien looked up and found Nora staring down at him in anger.

"Shh, she's sleeping."

"Nathaniel is coming. We cannot be divided."

"We won't. Look Nora, she almost collapsed. She needed to be held, Nathaniel will understand."

"You are glad I do." Nathaniel pulled form the shadows. "What happened exactly?"

"She felt her heart breaking."

"That means his heart was as well. Why the hell are they connected like that?" exclaimed Nathaniel.

"His majesty must have had a connection to that meddlesome white mage. I hate her," said Nora.

"Who cares, all I know is that Corbett needs to die, they all do," commented Damien.

They watched Luciana and soon Lucas came running in.

"What?" asked Nora.

"Bad news, and the good kind of bad that we like."

"What?"

"The elves, they are—"

"Are what?"

"Coming."

Nora growled and walked after him. "They should not come."

"Well it may not be that bad. They could be coming to join us," said Jason out of nowhere.

"They had better, I am in no mood to kill people." She looked up and noticed Esmerelda running toward her, her sword in hand.

"Their leader, he wants to kill Luciana." She laughed. "They're all dark elves, and to think, they wouldn't let *me* be queen. Anyway, the people, they say that thy will follow who ever lives."

"What's going on!" thundered Luciana voice.

A chill went down everyone back and they all looked at her frightened. Luciana walked down the stairs, her black dress flapped elegantly in her wake.

"A dark elf. He's come to . . . well to kill you," said Esmerelda. Damien laughed and Luciana smiled.

"I'll take care of this."

Luciana walked out calmly with Damien at her side. One elf stood in front many. He drew out his sword and Luciana drew back her head and laughed.

"What do you think you're going to do with that?"

"Take your place." He stabbed her and Luciana bent over acting as though she were hurt. Finally, she stood upright and pulled it out.

"Pathetic." She stabbed him and rose it up, slicing him vertically. She threw the sword to the ground and walked away.

"Damien, show them to where they belong." A shadow cast over her face as malevolence obscured all.

Chapter Eleven

S elene couldn't help but notice the fast recovery made by Nila. Not only did the antidote cure her, it healed her wounds as well. She rode her horse close to Arlis, a grim expression plastered on her face. She seemed to be avoiding Selene, making her think she had done something wrong. Edel was walking next to the horse and his presence made her smile. But in a way, he also seemed different. Arlis especially looked forlorn. He seemed sad and also tried to distance himself, not just from her, but from everyone.

"Edel, I think something is wrong. Did I do something wrong?" She felt like a child again, and it bothered her. She was supposed to be a fighter.

Edel simply gripped her hand and smiled. "Don't worry about it okay, they're just worried why Luciana wanted names. Just relax, it'll be fine." Selene nodded and couldn't help but smile. When she looked up, she noticed Nila staring back at her. Selene stared back frightened. She didn't know what to do.

Arlis stopped his horse and halted everyone.

"We'll leave the horses here," he said getting off his horse. "We'll walk into the village. Half now the rest later tonight. Two people of course will have to come here every so often to take care of the horses." He tied his horse to a tree and walked ahead of them. Nila followed suit and so did everyone else.

"I'll be one who comes to check on the horses horse," said Artemisa.

"So will I," said Nila.

Arlis nodded. "Edel, I want you to come with me, Selene, I want you coming after dark. You shouldn't be seen. Blake you too, come with me. Everyone else chose you're preference."

"Arlis why do I have to go now?" asked Edel who was helping a both frightened and confused Selene off her horse.

"Because I said so. Come on." He continued walking and Edel kissed Selene before walking away. Selene was confused but she sat on the ground nonetheless with those who stayed behind. She saw Artemisa's feet and looked up.

"What the hell what that all about?" Selene shrugged and pulled her knees to her chin. Artemisa sat down and hugged her. "You miss Edel already don't you?" Selene nodded sadly and thought herself a bit pathetic in nature for already missing him so. "Well don't worry, I'll take care of you." She smiled and Selene smiled back. She still didn't understand why Arlis was acting the way he was.

Her eyelids became heavy and she knew she should sleep but she was frightened. She didn't want to be plagued with another nightmare, or worse, another invasion of her mind. She couldn't help it thought, she laid her head back and closed her eyes.

*   *   *

Luciana flexed ger right hand. The hand she always had covered. She had cut all the finger extensions off, needing her talon like nails for her malevolent purposes. She looked back at the vial in her hand, and waited for Entia. Finally she arrived.

Her long flame red hair danced over her shoulders and elfin ears and her violent violet hateful eyes stared at Luciana who had yet to look up.

"Entia, what can you tell me about a crystal call the "Blue Light"?" she asked as she continued to flex her hand.

"What would you like to know," she asked taking a seat across from her.

"Everything I don't know already."

Entia stared at her, that was a difficult request. "Hmm, well I guess I'll just start with what I know. On another continent, there live dragons of five kind. They are the green, purple, silver, gold and crystal. Now it was said that the crystal dragon was and still is the purist dragon of them all. It would never lie, or be deceitful in any way, shape or form, even if it's own life depended on it. They say that a Crystal Dragon, one named Cedrus, took it upon himself and created a stone from a part of his heart and soul. It shines blue through all and it is known that who ever wields it can defeat any enemy. It was created to destroy darkness. They do however have a record of seeing it here, the people, but apparently it was stolen, it's value unknown to all. Why? Do you want it? Have you been searching for it?"

Luciana smiled and finally looked up. "I have no need to search for something that I already posses."

"What do you mean? You have it? You found it?"

"No Entia, I'm the one that stole it, all those centuries ago, that same night I found Damien." Finally she uncovered her hand. There embedded in her palm was the stone.

Entia's eyes widened in wonder. She couldn't believe what she was saying. "How—?"

"His dark majesty. It was part of my torture, it was my last physical torture. He found it and put it there, how do you think I was able to destroy his body?"

"So you've had that this entire time?" Luciana nodded. Entia couldn't help but let loose her outburst. "Then why haven't you killed any of them yet?"

"Because I find it more fun to play with them, their like my chess pieces." She laughed and Entia joined in.

"I never get tired of you Luciana. Now, what is the real reason you called me here. What do you need me to do?"

"Infiltrate another rebellion group, only not some mock band who don't know a thing about rebellion, I need you to find our lovely friends and infiltrate them."

"You're crazy!" exclaimed Entia. "They'll know it's me in a heart beat."

"Not if I give you a far more powerful potion than any other." She swung the vial in front of her face with two dainty fingers.

Entia ignored the vial and stared directly at her. "So you want me to find them?"

"Actually I want you to track down Donovan,"

Entia scoffed. "Why not send Adira, she simply loves doing that."

"He'll know it's her immediately, and only you have this natural talent for deceit and unadulterated hatred for Donovan."

"And with every right."

"My point is, track him down, find him, and infiltrate. Understood?"

"Of course. You want me to pray on his guilt."

"Good girl. Here," she said tossing the vial to her, "go have some fun."

Entia smiled. "Oh I plan to."

*　　*　　*

Corbett waited for Coryn to burst and yell and scream. Coryn was angry with him, he knew and waited patiently, like he would a pint of ale.

"I can't believe you! Why are you so idiotic! Why do you let your emotions get the better of you?! You always do this, you never think before you act!"

Corbett stared at her. "You are aware you're becoming annoying right?"

"Enough, hush, imbecile. Dammit Corbett have more self control!"

"Did I mention you're becoming annoying?"

"You've lived with me these past six-centuries so deal with it."

"Touchy today aren't you."

"Stop being so damn sardonic already." He sighed and rubbed his forehead. "You're an idiot."

"So I've been told."

"By whom?"

"Everyone, past and present."

"Why don't I doubt that."

Corbett laughed. "Because it's completely true. Everyone has said it at least once."

"Even Luciana?"

"Especially her." Why were they talking about her, he asked himself. He looked at Coryn who was staring at him intently.

"Just say it already, you know you want to."

Coryn looked towards the ground and then turned back to him. "You won't kill her will you?"

"Yes I will, I have to, to stop all of this. Everything."

"But do you have the strength to do so?"

Coryn didn't wait for an answer, he just walked ahead while Corbett stared at him aghast. He could do it, he would . . . unless he found another way to save the one he loved.

Corbett rubbed his eyes. He had to stop thinking about that, if he continued like that, he would never be able to kill her when the opportunity came.

He had to stop dwelling on the past. It served no purpose other than anguish. He took out his sword. The one Luciana had made for him with their friend Jason. Purest metal laced in magic. It had been made especially for him by two people who now wanted him dead. Two people he had grown up with, tow people he had shared almost everything with.

"Hey, are you all right," some one asked.

Corbett nodded and started walking ahead. He sheathed his sword. He knew that if he got rid of it, that would be the first real step to letting go, if only he wanted to let go.

"God I'm pathetic," he said to himself.

Someone pat him on the back. It was Cade. "No you're not . . . well only a little, bit it's perfectly normal."

Corbett laughed. "Right okay, it's perfectly normal to be immortal just to kill an old friend."

"Well when you put it that way, I see no normality whatsoever." Corbett looked at Cade. He knew what he was talking about, even if he had only been fighting this battle for a few years.. It was weird for him, being older than an elf, after all he was human.

"I envy you Cade."

"Why?"

"You're mortal, and an elf. You have wisdom. You probably wouldn't have made the same mistake I made."

Cade shook his head. "I probably would have. Everyone is weak Corbett, you can't fight that. Besides, as much as this pains me to say, we are all *human* on the inside." He shook the vile thought from his head and Corbett laughed.

"You elves, always so arrogant."

"Of course, do you expect anything less?" It was a rhetorical question but Corbett answered anyway.

"No, I wouldn't."

Cade and Corbett laughed. It was nice to laugh, but then again, it had been centuries since he laughed.

"So who really is Galen?"

"His real name is Donovan and he isn't really Trixies' cousin, his wife was though. He's a childhood friend we met on the road. He was an explorer I guess you could say. Sort of abandoned his daughter in the process. Trixie looked after her though."

"He had a daughter?"

Corbett nodded grimly. "General Entia."

*   *   *

Luciana examined Entia throughly. There could be no speck of her that could be recognized. Her red hair was now black and her lips were less full. Her cheek bones had changed somewhat, they were less defined, but her eyes remained almond shaped. Their colour remained violet though to remind him of what he lost. Only that shape remained and colour and those compared to everything else was nothing to cause suspicion.

"So am I ready to leave?" said Entia rather anxiously.

Luciana looked at her carefully. "Take a grey horse, one that doesn't look like it has been infected with darkness." She turned away then looked back and snapped her fingers in remembrance. "One more thing, control your anger, we don't need you to be exposed."

"How long will the potion last?"

"As long as I want. Now go."

Entia smiled in joy. Finally she got to have some fun. Rebellions were easy enough to infiltrate with the right story, but this one, the true one would be far more interesting. She walked to the stable and waiting for her was Adira, guiding a brown horse.

"I know she said grey but brown is less conspicuous. Besides, he liked brown horses, it'll make him keen to trust you if the others do not."

Entia took hold of the reins and climbed onto the horse.

"This is going to be fun Adira, I wish you could be there."

Adira growled. "So do I. Punch him for me will you."

"I'll do far more than that." Entia galloped away laughed.

In no time she reached the town. It was dusk and she looked around. No one was around, it was deserted, cold. She pulled up her hood and walked into the tavern and began to wait. According to Adira's last report, Donovan would be back here in a few days or so.

"Time to play daddy dearest."

Chapter Twelve

Selene woke up in Edel's arms with the suns rays upon her face. She sat up and looked down at the sleeping servant boy, her servant boy. Selene brushed a lock of hair out of his face and he shifted during his sleep only muttering the words 'I love you'. Selene couldn't fight her broad smile that took over her face.

Selene bent down to his ear and whispered. "I love you." Edel opened his eyes and stared at her dumbfounded.

"Selene . . ."

"Shh, come on lets go eat." She didn't need to hear anything from him, she already knew all she needed to know. She go dressed and she felt his eyes watch her.

When she looked back at him, he had his shirt already on and was fixing his boots on.

"Come on lets go."

He placed his hand on her lower back and led her out. Selene saw the warmth in his eyes as she descended the stairs.

"Edel can I ask you something?"

"Of course, what?"

"Why . . ." Selene was then interrupted by Nila's voice.

"Galen!"

Selene looked up and saw Nila run into the arms of a young man. He had soft brown hair and warm purple eyes. He must be — *liars* . . . Selene shook her head. Enough with the voices, she couldn't take it anymore. She walked down the stairs and toward them.

"Nila?"

She turned around and her face fell slightly.

"Selene this is Galen, my cousin." Selene extended her hand.

"Nice to meet you."

"The same, your friends talk so highly of your."

He laughed. "They should, or else I would think I was a bad leader." His laugh was like music and it made her smile. Entia heard him from behind her. The sound burned her ears but she stayed put, silent as she suffered.

"Well come, lets sit down." He led her to a seat, and sat down in front of her and ordered a pint of ale.

"So Selene, lets get to know each other." He smiled an angelic smile that made all her problems disappear. Luciana swore under her breath. It must be Donovan who was blocking her, protecting Selene, only he had this power.

*   *   *

Selene didn't like the look of the girl at the bar. For three days all she did was sit there, drink and eat. She really didn't like how her presence made her fell, she didn't, couldn't trust her. Finally, she slammed down her ale, spilling it on herself and the table and ignored the voices that called her as she walked over to the girl.

"Excuse me?" she said. The girl ignored her and continued drinking. Deep inside Entia smiled. Selene grabbed her arm and spun her around.

"I said excuse me."

"What do you want?" asked the girl rudely.

"I don't like you and I don't want you here."

"Not my problem." She turned back around, but Selene pulled her out of her seat and shoved her against the wall.

"Obviously you are understanding me. Leave."

"I paid for room and food, I have every right to be here, you have no right to tell me what to do."

"Selene!" She turned around and running to her was Galen.

Selene ignored him and shook her head. "No, I don't like her."

"Doesn't matter, you have no right to threaten her the way you are." Galen turned to the girl and she punched him. Far in the distance Adira smiled.

"Elfin scum! I did not need, nor did I want, your help!"

Galen stared at her strangely. He had never been talk to by that by regular village people. "What? Look I never did anything to you."

79

"You may not have, but your kind have. Allowing yourselves to be poisoned by the Queen. Your plants, your fruit, that you used to help feed my village, killed them! Your kind, you elves have given your army to her, you've let yourself become corrupt." She spit in his face.

"That can't be true," he said ignoring the spit that hit his face.

"But it is." She stormed from the tavern and Galen chased after her.

"Selene!" yelled Edel.

"What?"

"What the hell was that?!"

Selene was taken aback by his angry tone and fierce look but quickly regained herself. "I didn't like the way the air shifted around her. There is something not right about her."

Edels' face softened. "Selene, look, just relax all right. It doesn't matter if you like her or not, you had absolutely no right in which to act like that," said Edel looking away from her at the door.

Selene looked down ashamed. They were right, he was right, and she knew they knew she knew that they were right. She flexed her hands and looked up.

"Your right, I'm sorry."

Edel look back at her and took her in his arms rubbing her back. "Don't worry, come on lets just sit down and relax." Selene nodded and looked around. A shift in the air, eyes on her back, someone was watching her. Her eyes widened at the sight of Luciana, her black eyes piercing, holding a glass with her pale white marble like skin heightened by her black talons. Her black dress moved like waves as her leg danced up and down. Her marble like skin was revealed in the shift of each wave and her face, her beautiful dark evil face twisted into a smile. Selene blinked and her breathing failed her. She could feel herself fall to the ground, her eyes never leaving her until she was gone, as though she were never there.

*   *   *

Luciana laughed. No one but the pathetic puny princess had seen her. She laughed as he poured herself a glass of wine. Everything was pure hilarity, the girl had collapsed by the shock.

"Having fun," said two voices in unison. Luciana looked up. Adira and Nora stood together. Luciana brought the glass up to her lips and smiled a show of evil covering her eyes.

"Don't I always" she said before taking a sip. "The stupid princess collapsed when she saw me. It was hilarious, I had to leave before my laughter made me noticeable."

"How's Entia?" asked Adira.

"Oh she gave a spectacular performance. Her punch across Donovan face was brilliant and the spit in the face, beautiful." She laughed again and sat down.

"Hmm, you found this very amusing," commented Nora.

Luciana looked at her scrutinisingly. "You would to if you had witnessed what I witnessed." Adira sat down and poured herself a glass of wine.

"Hmm, I wish I had. Entia always did have a way with deceit. What story did she tell?"

"Elven kind have been corrupt and are piosoning the land. Donovan, or Galen rather, well lets just say, has already fallen under her spell. The princess mind you was a bit hard to manipulate. But that's partly due to Donovan presence." She laughed again and Nora leaned on the table, her blonde hair neatly fixed.

"So what exactly is the plan?"

"Come now, don't you like surprises?"

Nora raised an eyebrow. "Not particularly, but this one I think I may find enjoyable." She smiled and sat down.

Damien walked in, his ususal smirk on his face and leaned on the table arrogantly.

"I heard Entia is spying on Corbett and the rest of them. How's that going? Good?" He laughed. "Of course it is, I know. Anyway the reason I decided to grace you three with my presence is this, the stupid elves are kind of well, annoying, can't I kill them?" he wined.

"No," said Esmerelda storming in. "Sorry Luciana I have already told him that they are more valuable alive."

"And I said that they are annoying. Far to outspoken and idiotic. Constantly contradicting me because I am a half-elf. I swear I am going to murder them all."

Luciana put her drink down and circled the table. She draped her arm through his and looked at Esmerelda.

"Lets let him have some fun Esmerelda, there are a few who are a tad bit annoying. Besides Esmerelda, these are after all the same elves that denied you your crown, don't you want to have a little fun yourself?"

Esmerelda couldn't suppress her smile. "Well when you put it that way, I would love to join you."

*   *   *

Damien had not been over exaggerating. The elves were even refusing to do what she said because she was human, and concerning Esmerelda, they spat at her, calling her a disgrace to the kind, as though they had a right to talk. Luciana called and called for their attention but as they continued to ignore her, and her patience was beginning to run extremely low.

Luciana cast a spell that stilled the world. Some heads turned and she took that chance to grabbed a sword and kill an elf. Finally, she had all of their attention.

"Do I have your attention now? Good. You *will* obey me, or you will die, painfully slow, unlike this poor soul here. You will also obey my generals. Do as you're told or be tortured it's your choice, I've got the time for torture, I can and will always make the time for it." She gave the sword to Damien and walked back into the fortress. Stupid elves, she thought.

*　　*　　*

Corbett watched Selene. After her little outburst, she wanted some time be alone. Her outburst was unlike her, very unlike her. He drank his ale and someone tapped him on the shoulder. It was Coryn. He beckoned Corbett to follow him and hi did, leaving everyone with a potentially dangerous Selene.

Outside, were Trixie, Donovan and the girl you had punched him. She stood behind Donovan almost like a lost child.

"Everyone this is Líéd Telcia. She's from a village that resided on the outskirts of the elven Kingdom. Everything she said was unfortunately true. The elves have turned dark and are now part of her majesty's army. They pillaged her village and killed almost everyone, including her family."

Líéd kept her head to the ground and Corbett couldn't help but pity her. Selene had acted irrational.

"Líéd," began Trixie, "I know this may be hard, but did the elves ever say anything?"

She shook her head. "No, they just wanted to get to her, they had a leader, he said he was going to take her place; killed everyone who was in his way. He's dead now, she killed him."

"How do you know this?"

"Some of us, who survived were made into slaves, to feed them carry their weapons. I saw him stab her, with a sword. She simply took it out and sliced him in half. The generals saw us and let us go, said we were of no use to them dead or alive."

"That doesn't sound like them, letting people go like that," stated Trixie.

"Well think about it," began Coryn, "she has a whole army, add to that the newly annexed elven army; she has no use for peasants with no training."

"Her tactics are changing," said Corbett.

"And I don't like it," said Trixie. "I would have never seen this in a million years."

"Well lets think about it, she was gone for six centuries, stealing people here and there, keeping it undetected until she invaded with a mass army, she knows how to think on her feet," stated Coryn.

"Yeah, she always has," said Corbett bitterly.

"I hate that," commented Trixie.

"I wonder what she has up her sleeves now," commented Donovan.

"Are you going to stop her?" asked Líéd.

"We're going to try," said Donovan.

"Thank you." Donovan smiled and took her in his arms like he would a daughter, his daughter. He led Líéd into the inn and Corbett watched them go. He couldn't understand why Selene disliked her, there was nothing wrong about her.

"I don't like this Corbett," said Trixie all of a sudden.

He looked down at her. "Why not?"

"Luciana, she's . . . I don't like what I sense. There is a reason for Selene's outburst today, I know it."

"Luciana."

She nodded. "She's manipulating her mind."

"I thought that was already established."

"I'm going inside, to take care of Selene. Don't dwell on it Corbett."

She walked away but her words stuck in his brain. He could not help but dwell on it; ever since Luciana took control, she was all he ever thought about, and now her effect on Selene. and his foolish emotions were becoming a hassle.

"Corbett, she's right, don't' dwell over it, it's really all you ever think about. I mean I don't blame you, I really don't but you should, oh never mind I'm not making any sense." Coryn sighed and Corbett laughed when he walked away. He remembered when he met him and his sister, and after all these years, he hadn't changed.

Corbett was walking down the road of the town, leaving Luciana to wander around. She was exhausted, and just wanted air. Then, while looking around he saw, the beautiful princess, and he couldn't help but stare at her transfixed. He took a flower from a vendor while he wasn't looking and took a step but stopped short and looked down at the flower. Corbett scoffed at himself, pretty girls did not fall for cheap parlour tricks. He tossed it to the ground and stepped on it in his wake.

"Uh hello." The princess turned and he saw it a sword at her belt as well as a pouch, like Luciana. "You're a warrior-mage!"

She smiled and the cold hardness in her eyes vanished and was replaced by warm curiosity.

"Warrior yes, mage not so much. Now who are you?" she had asked looking him up and down admiringly.

"My name is Corbett, I'm well a thief I guess, didn't care what I did as long as I kept my family fed."

She smiled. "Hmm, that's sweet, in a way. My name is Nora and my brother . . ." She turned around then growled under her. "Coryn, you insolent brat to the throne, where have you gone?"

"Wait, did you say throne?" he asked in false surprise, he didn't think it would be good to tell her that her disguise was pitiful . . . in the meantime anyway.

Nora looked at him frightened, then smiled tenderly. "Allow me to clarify, I am Princess Nora, mage in training, I'm half decent, and my brother is Prince Coryn, heir to the throne and supposed warrior," she added with a bit sad regret.

"What are you doing out of the palace?"

"Fighting for our kingdom," said a voice. Behind him was a young man eating an apple. He smiled at him, then as quick as a snake, Nora knocked the apple from his hand and gripped his wrist twisting it.

"You brat, I was worried about you. Don't you dare do that again, how the hell do you plan to protect yourself?" He looked at her blankly then down at the apple.

"Ow let go of me and hello I was eating that." Nora let go of him and Corbett laughed.

"It's nice to meet you Prince Coryn, I'm Corbett."

"Please, call me Coryn, I don't really care for the prince title outside the palace anyway. But then again there I have no choice." He looked between them. "So what's going on?"

"I was talking to your sister. You said you are fighting for your kingdom correct." Coryn nodded. "That's brilliant, you can help me then! My friends and I are sort of bent on this quest I guess you could say, to stop *him*. Will you join us, we could use all the help we can get?"

"Of course! As prince I must do everything in my power to stop him and . . . wow I lost my thought there." He laughed and Nora rolled her eyes and crossed her arms. "This happens to me a lot."

"Behold, our future king." Nora laughed and hugged her brothers shoulders. "Honestly, though I can't think of a better candidate for a ruler." She kissed him on the cheek and clasped her arm through his and looked at Corbett warmly.

"We would love to join you, I don't think we could defeat *him* by ourselves anyway. Meet us in the tavern, we will be there waiting." She smiled and they walked away. As they did, Corbett heard Coryn say, "you are going to replace that apple right?" Nora laughed.

"Of course I am, you're my little brother, it's *my* job to care of you, above everything. After all, if I didn't who would." She kissed his cheek/

Corbett looked at the tavern, he felt bad for Coryn. He had lost far more than a sister, he had also lost his best friend.

Chapter Thirteen

Luciana paced the tower of her room, her porcelain skin reflected the darkness around her. Finally she snapped and knocked all her potions and concoctions to the ground and shattered all the glass making it bounce off her skin. She couldn't help but be furious, the stupid pathetic princess had his heart, or part of it anyway. Her plan was slowly falling to pieces and if Entia failed, nothing would work. She bit down on her onyx stone nails and once again threw a glass against the wall. A shard imbedded itself in her neck and she swore as she pulled it out. The bleeding was not ceasing. Luciana sat down calmly and let the blood drip down her neck, it's not like it would kill her, nothing could, unless the curse was broken, and he would never figure out a way to stop it, not in time anyway.

A drop of blood hit the floor but she remained a statue. Her nails sank deeper into the chair as she stared around the place. What was the point of immortality of no one would be there to remember me? Stop it, yelled a voice in her head, they will all remember you, you are Luciana, the Dark Empress. A satisfied smile slowly appeared on her face and she slowly stood up. Now one would ever forget her, not again, not ever.

Luciana waved her hands in the air and cleaned up all the mess. That was how she always cleaned everything, ever since she was sixteen and had become a master at the blood-lined trade, which was why she was the star child even though she caused trouble in her wake, and always with Corbetts' help.

"Corbett, Luci, come on we shouldn't be doing this," said a thirteen year old Isabelle wide eyed with fright.

"That's why we wanted you to stay home Bella," said Luciana, taking off her robe.

"Yeah, Bella," said Corbett. "Look we need the money, stealing this and selling it to the thieves will help with money."

"But . . ."

"Enough little sis, besides this will be great practice for my magic." She flexed her fingers anxiously.

"If mom and dad . . ."

"If mom and dad find out they'll be proud because I used my magic and because this is the only way to help. And besides I unlike you took the time to learn what they taught me, instead of running off every time to play with my bow and arrow."

Isabelle clasped her hands over her ears and shook her head. "SHUT UP!"

"Why should I, if you ever listened to them you would make them proud and learn much more. Now stay here and keep an eye out, you see anyone send an arrow at me."

Isabelle had her head down. "What if I hit you?"

Luciana smiled and lifted her little sisters chin meeting her eye to eye warmly. "Don't worry about that, just fire." She kissed her on the head and hugged her tightly. "Everything will be much better after this, I promise."

Isabelle nodded. "Okay."

Luciana snuck off with Corbett and he pulled her aside.

"Don't you think you were a little harsh on her?"

"No. Look, she ran off again yesterday and you know how my mom usually feeds the entire village?" Corbett nodded. "Well she gets the strength to do that because she's so angry at Isabelle for running off . . . again. Well yesterday we had no food. I was up in my room and I hard a door slam and who should I see running from the house from my window but Bella. Then next thing I go is run downstairs and I see my mother. She looked completely mad, I mean she was slamming all the cupboards looking for food. I just stand aside, in the shadows of the door watching her. We had no food Corbett, none. You should have seen her, when that realization dawned on her, she fell to the ground and collapsed into tears. My dad ran in and held her and I just stood there and watched. I've never seen her cry Corbett, it angered me." Luciana was shaking, releasing that moment her mother was crying, made her grow so furious that all she could do was shake.

Corbett grabbed her hand and laced his fingers through hers. Luciana looked up at him and smiled as he smiled down at her.

"Come on Luci, lets go make everything all right."

They ran off together, hand in hand. They had not been caught, she had broken the glass with a spell making no sound. They had stolen priceless items and had taken a trip to Vestry, The City of Thieves, and thankfully, Luciana had cast charms to protect their items as well as sell them. Their parents had not asked where the money had come from, they already knew, but they had praised them anyway, and for a short time, life was better.

Luciana opened her green eyes and opened her tower door and walked gracefully down the steps.

"Insolent brat," she muttered projecting her breath to Isabelle's Tavern.

Isabelle dropped the glass she was holding and swore. She hated hearing her sisters voice, and now she was hearing it more frequently then ever. Two feet appeared in front of her as she picked up the glass. She already knew who it was. She looked up into her friends autumn honey eyes.

"Hello Toad." She got up and stared at him. She knew that wasn't his real name, but she couldn't help but humour him.

"Are you all right?"

"Yes, it just slipped. I've been being a slight butter fingers lately." She laughed, drawing him away from her carelessness. "It's all right, don't worry."

"Uh huh, why don't I believe you Bella?"

"Because you are you."

He smiled. "That's right. Now tell me, what's wrong?"

"I've just been a little on edge lately, I don't know why, it's just I have been."

He took her in his arms and she laid her head on his chest and listened to his heart beat. It felt nice to listen to the beating heart of someone she loved. A pang hurt her heart and she pushed herself away from Toad. She felt him look at her in confusion and pain and she knew the were all watching her as she ran from her own tavern.

Isabelle stood alone, in her secret place where she caused everything. Where she had killed the two people she loved more than anything.

Isabelle was saying a spell over the food she was cooking. She would not let more people die, she would not let them go after His Royal Darkness just to see if her sister was alive.

"Isabelle you need to stop this," said a voice. Isabelle stopped casting her spell and stood up frightened. Behind her stood Nathaniel.

"You don't understand," she began trying to explain. "I have to, if Corbett goes to save her we all will, and she's dead."

He looked at her angrily. "You don't know that, besides we need to keep out promise!"

"We promised nothing! Corbett did!"

"She's your sister."

"I know, but she's dead Nathaniel, I know she is," she said clutching her heart. "There is no reason for him to bother keeping her alive."

"There is also no reason for why he took her."

"She's dead Nathaniel, and when he comes after us, I swear I will kill him, I will avenge my sister."

The stood tehre across eash other. Isabelle frightened of him and Nathaniel angry and confused. Finally Nathaniel sighed and looked at her.

"You have to tell them what you have been doing . . . before I do, and *I* promised Isabelle, I will, when this battle is over."

Isabelle stood shocked and angry. He had no right, he couldn't betray her like that, they were supposed to be in love. All of a sudden Corbett ran into the small clearing and stared at Isabelle. She stared back at him and took in his appearance. He was dishevelled and looked beaten, broken.

"Corbett, what happened?" asked Nathaniel before Isabelle could utter a word.

"Luciana's alive." Isabelles' eyes widened as she felt her insides collapse, she couldn't breath.

"What?" she managed to ask.

"She's alive, I knew she was. Why . . ." Corbett said dazed, looking at his hands.

"Corbett," said Nathaniel angrily, "start form the beginning, what happened?"

"I was with Nora and Luciana was just there sitting in midair, in black. She said she killed *him* and I knew she was telling the truth. She killed him and became him. She killed Nora, turned her into an un-dead soldier."

Isabelle collapsed to the ground. Oh god, what have I done, she thought. "This can't be happening.," she stammered as she began to cry. Corbett hugged her and she looked up at Nathaniel. He stared down at her more in disgust than in anger.

She didn't know what she was doing. She saw Nora battling her little brother. She saw Esmerelda stabbed in the heart, but not die. She saw her sister walking arrogantly calm in the mass chaos, toward Corbett. Isabelle pulled out an arrow and aimed it at her sister who paid her no heed.

Someone called her name. It was Nathaniel. She turned and watched him. He was outnumbered, he would die if she did not intervene. She turned her arrow toward the heart of the soldier at his side.

"You disgust me." He had said that to her when she had begged him not to breath a word. She shot the arrow unknowingly and stood there stunned.

"What have I done." They stopped attacking Nathaniel and also stared at the arrow embedded in his heart. Nathaniel dropped his sword and pulled the arrow out. She watched as he fell to the ground and stared at the arrow. She started to run to him but stopped short. Luciana appeared in front of him, her back to her. She kissed him and Isabelle saw her nail sink into his neck as she stabbed him and suddenly his wounds healed and he wasn't dying anymore.

Luciana never turned to her, just walked over to Corbett who was to distracted to notice her presence. She looked back at Nathaniel who was walking to her coldly. Isabelle backed up with her eyes teary.

"Nathaniel, I—I–I d-didn't, you have to believe me, I love you."

"Just like you loved your sister? And wow, would look at how that turned out." He lashed his sword at her and she stumbled back and pulled out her sword.

"Nathaniel please, listen to me."

"No."

Isabelle heard a twig break, and jerked around, dagger in hand. Out came Toad, behind the trees. Isabelle rolled her eyes and sheathed her dagger.

"Dammit Toad, don't sneak up on me like that."

"What's wrong Bella?"

"I haven't been sleeping well."

"It's more than that, I can tell. Now tell me Bella."

I can't!" She stared at him. She was sick of lying to the people she loved and saw down on a rock.

"Toad, I need t tell you something. Sit down please."

Toad looked at her curiously and sat down next to her. Isabelle would tell him everything, including what she did.

"Okay what do you need to tell me."

She smiled and took his hand in hers. "Toad, my name is Isabelle Sanluida, my sister is Luciana Sanluida, her unholy majesty and I am six hundred and seventy-six years old . . ."

Chapter Fourteen

Entia sipped her pint of ale slowly. So far everything was going as planned. Donovan was close to her like a father to a daughter, of course he would fell a compulsion to act like a father, especially towards a someone who has watched her father murdered.

"Do you want something to eat," he asked.

"No, I'm fine, I'm not really hungry."

"You haven't been hungry in a while."

"I don't really have much of an appetite, watching people get slaughtered kind of killed it." She smiled faintly and drank her ale again. Your pathetic Donovan. He wrapped his arm around her and Entia was taken back as well as very disgusted. She didn't want him touching her, she wanted him dead and by her hand.

"Are you all right?" he asked.

"I'm fine, just a little sick to say the least."

"Maybe you should get some rest, some sleep."

"If you're sure." He smiled and she walked off to her room, relieved.

"Having fun!" asked a voice.

Entia leaned on the door and looked at Adira who sat on her bed.

"He touched me, I hated it before I turned and I hate it now, more than ever." She shivered and threw her cloak onto the floor.

"Hmm."

"What hmm?"

"Well he feels guilty, how pathetic." She laughed.

"It is isn't it I can't believe she wants me to do this. I hate being around them all of them, their . . that white witch's power, it's sickening."

"I can imagine. Entia do you think they suspect, that you are not what you seem, what you say?"

"Uh, no." She laughed. "This potion is too powerful, it even alludes my power, his power." She sat on the dresser and stared at Adira. "How's Luciana?"

Adira growled. "You remember how he took up magic, well his power is amplified by *her* and well, he is interfering with her influence so, she is not well." She pulled out a tiny vial. "We want you too feed this the Selene. It will allow Luciana to influence her without interference."

Entia took it, and looked at the contents closely. "I don't want to know what's in this do I?"

Adira thought about it. "Hmm, no you don't."

"How vile?"

"Very. Live things were put into it to say the least."

Entia smiled. "Disgusting, yet strangely aesthetic."

"Of course you would think so."

"Don't you?"

Adira smiled, then it faded. "He's coming. He must sense me."

"Quick, throw me against the wall, choke me. Act as though you're questioning me, quick." Adira grasped her neck and lifted her above the ground. Then, as expected, Donovan burst through the door and with him Trixie. Adira dropped Entia to the ground and stared at him.

"Lucky her, for many reasons." She disappeared and Entia gasped for air. Damn Adira had a grip.

"Líead are you all right?" asked Donovan holding her. Get off me, she screamed in her head.

"I'm fine. She just wanted information of a man named Donovan. I tried to tell her I knew nothing but she didn't, wouldn't listen."

"Who the hell is Donovan," said Trixie, convincingly. Entia wanted to laugh but held back. Pathetic fools, don't' you know, can't you sense. The white magic suddenly flew up her nostril and she began to cough uncontrollably. Donovan and Trixie stared at her worried or she pushed herself away from them and toward a window. Air she needed air. She needed them away from her, now.

"Are you—"

"I-I'm fine. Please, ju-just leave, I would—like some time alone." She couldn't see, she was passing out. This always happened to her, she had always been a frail child. Now, all was black and as she fell into unconsciousness she heard Donovan call her by her true name and she smiled victoriously.

*   *   *

Donovan wet a piece of cloth and put in over Líéad's forehead. She looked so fragile, so scared, so alone. Her family had been taken from her, killed slaughtered in front of her face, leaving her broken, like Entia. She had been strong, until he left. He loved her, there was no doubt that he did, she was his daughter but he had wanted to leave. He had wanted to go away, and taking his daughter would never have been allowed, traditional; and time after time he had tried to tell Entia that, but she never listened, she always said that if he had truly ever loved her, he would have taken her, no matter what and deep down, he knew she was always right.

"You called her Entia," said Trixie suddenly.

"I know."

He heard Trixie sigh. Her hand was on his shoulder. "Donovan you cannot replace your daughter."

"I'm not trying to. It's just, she's so frail, so broken, just like her."

"Not to offend you but that's your fault. You left her, when you could have, and should have taken her."

"It wasn't allowed."

"I would have allowed it, Esmerelda would have, you but didn't even bother to ask, you just left her with us after her mother died. You just left."

"I visited."

"Not often."

"What are you talking about, I would come back every few months and would always send a letter."

"Months turned into years Donovan. You missed when she became a Ranger, building herself to be all that she could. You missed her grow up."

"I saw enough of it, he retorted.

Trixie shook her head rudely. "No you didn't. Do you know what she would do, whenever you sent a letter, she would open it, read it by the fire and then toss it in while she said, "you don't love me, if you did you would have taken me, not abandoned me". And then after she would run off into the forest for days at a time crying." Trixie looked away from him and stared at Líéad, she was fragile, just like Entia. She looked back at Donovan sadly. "She wanted a father Donovan, not just letters to falsify the ideal of one.

"You know Donovan, I remember the day there was no letter, no "I love you" or "love your father". That day started out as the most wonderful day of her life. She was proposed to and she was finally going to write to you herself. Then she came back, told us the good news and asked for the letter you sent. Our faces fell Donovan and in that instant she knew that there was no letter, that you had sent nothing, absolutely nothing.

"Entia ran out in that beautiful purple dress of hers that matched her eyes. She ruined it by hiding amongst the trees for days, those trees she as so connected with . . . they hid her well. We couldn't find her. For days she was gone, and she would have stayed hidden had she not stumbled upon Corbett and Luciana intruding into the land. She didn't even stay, she ran off with them and Esmerelda. You hurt her Donovan, she was so beautiful, so alive not just broken, until you destroyed her, you left her shattered in pieces."

There was nothing that he could say, she was right and her knew it deep inside. He had hurt her beyond belief, braking her. "I didn't mean to. I wanted to surprise her by coming back and staying."

Trixie crossed her arms. "Well you couldn't have picked a more inopportune time."

"I know."

"And then when you ran into them on their journey, Esmerelda told me Entia punched you and screamed at you and told you that you were dead to her."

"Esmerelda told you the truth."

"I thought as much."

Donovan couldn't take anymore. He knew what he had done. "Trixie can you just go get me some more hot water?"

"Of course."

Donovan watched her leave. Entia had always been frail, strong but frail nonetheless. Always had coughed spasms which frequently caused her to pass out. He remembered when he saw her on the road. His daughter all grown up. She had been helping Isabelle perfect her archery skill and he had given her a hug from behind. She not only punched him, she threw him to the ground, and when everyone asked who he was she had told them that it was her father. But confusion had recked their brains and someone had said that she had told them that he was dead.

"To me he is," she had said as she walked away.

"I'm sorry Líead for what the elves took from you." He saw her eyes flicker and fist clench. He kissed her forehead and she relaxed a bit.

*　　*　　*

Entia was dreaming, remembering. Her fathers presence was making her ill at ease. They stopped for camp for a day or two, hoping to catch their breath.

"Entia."

"Do not talk to me," she said ignoring him.

"I'm your father—"

"No your not!" She screamed as she stared ta him angrily, with her fist clenched, ready to punch him again. "A father would not have abandoned his daughter. He would have taken her no matter what the cost!"

They just stared at each other among the stares of the crowd. A twig broke and Entia pulled out her arrows and they all stared at the forest. Emerging forth was none other than Adira.

"Adira?" questioned Entia putting away her arrow.

"Entia, oh my I thought that was your who screamed." She giggled and embraced her in a hug. Entia was stiff but hugged her back and smiled.

"Adira what are you doing here?"

"Trixie sent me, she wants me to bring you back home, back where you belong, back to Silkas."

"I can't."

"What do you mean you can't?"

"I have to do this."

"You have to do nothing, except come home and marry my brother."

"I will come back."

"We want you to come back now, you will die if you don't," she said hushed. "Your condition is well—"

Entia ignored her comment about her condition. "You know for someone who is suppose to be two centuries older than me, you can be far younger then me."

Adira smiled sweetly. "Someone has to, you're far to serious . . . Entia please come back."

"I can't."

Adira stared at her frustrated then finally crossed her arms and planted her foot into the ground playfully, finally submitting to Entia's will. "Fine, but I'm coming and so is Trixie."

"What," said Donovan, Esmerelda and Entia in unison.

Adira smiled. "If I don't return, which I'm not, she's coming and by the look of things, you'll need us."

"Well welcome," said Corbett suddenly.

Entia jerked up and was faced with reflection. She looked around. He had called her by her name, not her alias. Her frailty had reminded him of her.

"Idiot." She took her feet off the bed and sat up. The vial, she finally remembered. She searched all around the room, but couldn't find it. She got down on the hands and knees and searched every crevice of the floor. If they found it, they would know who she really was. She would have woken with them surrounding her. She crawled under her bed and sighed in relief. It was in a crack. She used her nails to pry it out and clasped it in her hand.

"Líead?" asked a voice. Entia jerked and hit her head on the frame of the wooden bed. She swore under her breath and stuffed the tiny vial in her shirt.

"Yes?" she said coming up. Standing at the door was Selene with two trays of food in her hands.

"Are you all right, I thought I'd bring you some food, to be hospitable. It wasn't right how I treated you when we first met."

Perfect, she thought. "It's all right, you have all the right to be hostile, I would have."

"Yes well, I know how it feels to have your entire world striped away from you." She set the food down and sat.

"Yes you do, more than anyone I guess. Thank you for the food."

"You're welcome. Uh, do you mind if I eat with you I feel like you're the only person who understands." Entia held back the laughter inside her. She understood nothing, and neither did she care.

"I understand. Go get some drinks, I'll set up a table." Entia smiled sweetly and so did Selene. Once she as gone Entia massaged her jaw, she was not used to smiling so honestly and sweetly.

Entia moved her junk off the dresser and brought one chair to one side and another, one she found stationed outside her door, to the other side. Selene returned and set down the pints of ale and sat

"Formal introductions. My name is Selene, I was, am the princess."

"Líead Telcia, I was the daughter of the Major. Now I'm only one the few survivors."

"I'm so very sorry."

"Don't be, it's not your fault. You didn't do anything for her to be so cruel, to ruin lives."

"I know, but I feel sorry because I know how it feels to lose family. To be so alone."

"Hmm." She ate some potatoes and licked her lips. They were nicely seasoned. Selene drank some of her beer and smiled a thought.

"Did you have a little brother Líead?"

"Twins, two little ones who always got into all sorts of mischief."

"My little brother one time during dinner while my parents were fights, you see they fought a lot since he was born, they walked into another room and my older sister threw some food at me and I threw some back at her and we were so busy throwing food at each other that neither of us noticed that he got into our parents wine and drank it. Our parents were so furious, we were after all nobility we should've acted like it."

Entia laughed, not because the story touched her but because the princess was falling into her trap. Entia stole a glance at her glass and smiled.

"Selene, you're glass is half empty, and so is mine, here let me go refill them."

"Huh, oh okay." Entia smiled and grabbed both of their glasses and walked from the room and down the stairs back down to the bar. She placed the pint glasses in the bar and asked for a refill and inconspicuously pulled the vile from her shirt.

With the return of the goblets she quickly poured the contents into Selene's goblet.

"I don't get paid enough to do this," she said carrying them back to the room. She heard Luciana laughed. "Of course you think it's funny." Luciana laughed even more.

"I'm back."

"Huh, oh thanks."

"She has to finish it Entia," said Luciana's voice. Entia rolled her eyes and placed Selene's glass in front of her.

"So aren't the potatoes delicious?"

"I love them," said Selene. She took a gulp of her drink and Entia tensed. Selene just put the goblet back down and went back to eating.

Entia smiled. "Selene, can I ask you something?"

"Of course?"

"Do you ever get the feeling that you are being watched?"

"All the time." She drank another huge gulp from her drink. "My god these are spicy," she laughed.

Entia smiled. "I know, I love them."

Selene laughed and ate some of the chicken then finished the last of her drink.

"Líead can you go get Edel, I'm a tad bit drunk," she laughed and Entia smiled.

"Of course."

Líéad went for him and looked at all her old friends and new enemies. "Edel, Selene is drunk, she needs you to carry her back to her room."

He looked at her curiously. "What? Oh well okay then." He followed her back to her room, and there was Selene, passed out on the table. Entia covered her mouth to keep from laughing and helped Edel carry Selene back to her room.

Alone in her room at last, Entia finished the last of her food, blew out her candles and went to bed.

"Idiots," she muttered aloud as she closed her eyes.

Chapter Fifteen

S elene, wake up," called a distant voice. She opened her eyes, and hovering over her was Edel. She smiled and stretched. How drunk had she gotten with Líead, she mused. Edel pulled her close and she drank in his scent. He didn't smile like ale and food, he smiled like he always did, a sweet scent, and she loved that. She lifted her head and once again he wasn't there, he was somewhere else, someplace else. His black hair was dishevelled and his eyes were sad.

"Edel?"

"Yes?"

"Where are you?"

He looked at her and smiled. "Here with you of course."

"Physically yes, but mentally, where are you, what are you thinking about?"

He looked at her then back towards the ceiling. "War," he said calmly.

"Her army out numbers us, twenty to one, maybe even more."

"Yeah. Selene . . ."

"Yes?"

"I . . . I'm hungry, do you want me to bring you some food?"

Selene's face fell. "Yes, whatever they have and some water, my head hurts from last night."

"So I would expect," he laughed and began out the room and she forced a smile. He was going to say it back, she just knew that he was.

"Servant boy," she mused to herself, meaning to demean him.

"Who's a servant boy," came a voice. Standing at the doorway was Artemisa. Her long wavy hair bounced in the sunlight.

Selene mustered up a faint smiled. "Edel."

"Oh, why are you calling him such a degrading title?"

"Because he chickened out and didn't say he loved me."

"Oh." Artemisa laughed and Selene threw a pillow at her head. "Hey that was un-called for, really, and besides, you have to admit it is funny."

"No it's not. I've said it twice already. I just—"

Artemisa closed the door behind her and leaned against it frustrated and amused. "Be patient, my god, you're ridiculous really. Look he's Edel, you know he's always been shy, you were the one who kissed him first after all. Just relax, he'll say it all in due time."

Selene sighed and covered herself with the covers blocking out the rays of the sun. She felt Artemisa climb in the bed to join her.

"I really do love him," said Selene after a few moments of silence.

"I know you do. Selene can I tell you a secret?"

"Of course."

"I like Blake . . . a lot."

"Really?"

Artemisa nodded. "He's so . . . perfect, and knowledgeable."

"How long have you known him?"

"A while, before I met you. You know at first I didn't like you, I thought you swept him away from me."

"Artemisa!" she exclaimed.

"This was before I met you rememberer, besides, I was wrong, and you were a nice person.

"Oh, well thank you, I think you're a nice person too." Selene giggled and Artemisa kicked her from under the covers.

"I think you're still a tad bit drunk."

Worry struck her. "I didn't do anything crazy did I?"

"Actually you did. You got up on the bar and started to dance and all other sorts of things, including professing your love for Edel."

Selene gasped and sat up straight, pulling the soft warm quilt along with her. Her eyes were wide and Artemisa started to laughed hysterically.

"Oh my, you should see your face! It's priceless!" She made a mock expression and went back to clutching her stomach as she laughed. "You weren't that drunk Selene, really I was making it up!"

Selene slanted her eyes, took her pillow and began attacking her friend, nearly knocking her off the bed.

"That was a rotten thing to do Artemisa Dermo."

"Oh I couldn't resist, besides it got your mind off Edel didn't it?" Selene stopped with her arm holding the pillow in mid air.

"Yes, I guess you did." She put the pillow down and Artemisa sat up.

"What, no thank you?"

"I stopped hitting you didn't I?" She laughed and hugged her friend. "Thank you."

"Anytime." Artemisa returned the hug and got out of the bed. "Well, I'll leave you to your rest." She turned and walked away then turned back to her. "I find it odd though that after two pints you were drunk Selene."

Selene stared ta her confused. "I only had two?"

Artemisa nodded. "Yes, you have a weak stomach I must say." She laughed and walked form the room, closing the door behind her.

Selene sat there in bed and crossed her legs. She didn't have a weak stomach, she could always drink more than two pints and hold her own ale. So either the ale was stronger than back home or something was put into her drink.

"Líead," she hissed. She jumped from her bed and ran to Líead's room in her under garments. The bed was fixed and empty and Selene clutched her head and fell to the ground. A sound penetrated her head as she collapsed to the ground.

Luciana would not let her figure out her plan, she simply wouldn't. She plucked the thought from her head and ended her spell. Donovan had no power anymore she sneered.

Selene shook her head and looked around. What was she doing in Líead's room, she asked herself. She stood up and looked around.

"Selene?" Someone asked. Selene turned around and stared at Líead.

"Hi, uh, I don't know why I'm here, to be quite honest."

"Oh, hmm, are you feeling well?" asked Líead.

"A little light headed, but other than that I feel great." She laughed and Líead just smiled.

"I'm glad you feel fine, come down, we were just starting to eat breakfast."

"Really? Oh Edel was suppose to bring me breakfast in bed."

"Come on, wouldn't you rather have breakfast with your friends than just Edel?" Líead gave her a warm smile and Selene caved. Why not, she asked herself.

"Okay, sure, yeah, just let me put some clothes on." She smiled and ran back to her room, why had she been in Líead's room. She slipped on her blouse and a pair of shorts then tied on her brown boots. She quickly brushed her hair and tied it up then for a moment felt compelled to stare at her reflection.

Luciana saw in her eyes the beginnings of a darkness, whether or not she herself was the cause of it, she was unsure, but whatever it was, Luciana liked it. She flexed her fingers and her talons erupted, only instead of being black they were jade, just like her eyes. She swore and released her hold on Selene, letting her walk from the room, none the wiser of Luciana's power.

"You have far to much fun playing with your new toy," said a sultry voice. Luciana turned and saw Nathaniel behind her. His black armour reflected the green glow of her talons.

"Well I must, I enjoy my new found power over her I mean one must enjoy themselves shouldn't one?"

"Yes one must." He laughed and she smiled. He talons turned black and her smiled broadened. She walked over to him and kissed him. Nathaniel took her in his arms roughly and pulled her close.

"Oh enough you two," someone said hotly. It was Nora. "We need to focus. Who is keeping a tab on the princess?"

"Entia of course," said Luciana.

"But what if she needs you? What about the princess hmm?"

"What about her!" screamed Luciana angrily. She took a deep breath then quickly regained herself. "Entia will take care of her as long as she stays close or gives her something of her, I don't always have to be watching, now shoo." She resumed her kissing of Nathaniel but Nora pulled her away and dragged her from the room, slamming her against the wall. Luciana stared at her calmly. She must have lost her mind, she thought.

"This is no time for fooling around. You need to stay away from all of it, until you . . . you know, until you bear Corbetts child."

"So what do you want?" she said shoving Nora off her.

"Go to the fortress. It's the safest thing to do, for all of us, for the plan."

Lucian thought it over and finally came to the conclusion that Nora was right. When it came to Corbett all she wanted was him, nothing else mattered but him, not even her revenge mattered at times.

"Okay, fine, you win, I'll go to the fortress." And with that she was gone, at her true palace. She traced her hands over the stone walls and walked up to the tower at the top. The stones seemed to welcome her touche as she felt a slight tingle throughout the walls.

"I'm home, she said to herself as she overlooked her desolate kingdom.

*　　*　　*

Entia was en enjoying herself far too much but then again fooling all her enemies and being a spy was immensely amusing. She sat next to the princess and ate her breakfast while the others babbled on. So far no one talked about the coming battle so of course yet there was nothing to report to Luciana so all she could do was be a spy and play her part as she saw fit, which was becoming mundane.

"Líead, how are you," said Trixie out of nowhere.

Oh god, thought Entia. "I'm fine, how are you?"

"Oh all right. Say, how many drinks did Selene have last night?" Her tone was full of suspicion and her eyes shined with distrust.

"She had already been drinking when she came up so I'll estimate about four to six total. However much she had down here plus two."

"Hmm—" The suspicion was gone and Trixie smiled warmly. Well anyway, your appetite seems to have improved, I'm glad."

"So is D—" Entia began to choke on her food as Luciana's grip clamped down on her throat. She noticed the darkness, but no one else did.

"Galen, Entia," she hissed before letting her go to spit up her food.

"Oh my god, Líead, are you all right?"

"Yes, fine, the food just went down the wrong way, don't worry I'll be fine."

"Okay, if you're sure. Now what were you saying?"

"Galen is happy that my appetite has improved as well."

"Oh well, we all are, your health means a lot to us, especially considering what you have been through."

"Huh, oh, yeah, I try not to think about it."

"I don't blame you. I lost family. My older sister and my niece and a man whom I loved and had hoped to marry. She took them away from me."

"I'm so sorry for your loss. How long ago?"

Trixie looked at her. "Long enough. Don't let your anger consume you, it's effects are dangerous." She kissed Entia on the head before leaving. Selene popped up next to her and Líead wanted to smack her.

"What was that about?"

"Tri-Nila, she just wanted to make sure that I was okay. She's glad my appetite had improved."

"Well it is good, we're all glad."

She smiled. "Luciana," she called. Her mind was swept away to a dark horizon.

"Yes?"

"What do you want me to give her?"

"Here," she said tossing her a silver bracelet with but one onyx stone. "Tell her it was a gift from your little brothers and that you feel like she could be a sister. Or something sentimental like such."

Entia looked it over. "This will give me partial control over her?"

"Only partial."

Entia held the bracelet under the table. She had no idea what the princess was babbling on about, nor did she care.

"Selene," she said finally getting a word in. "I want you to have something. My brother made it for me with help from the elves and I want you to have it," She handed her the bracelet and Selene stared at it shocked.

"Oh my Líead I can't."

"No, I want you to. Please take it."

"If it means that much to you, I will. Líead thank you."

"Lets say it's from both of our brothers to us."

"Líead thank you." A tear fell down her cheek and surprisingly enough, down Líeads' as well. She looked at her father who turned away smiling as she hugged Selene.

Luciana wiped away the lone tear that had also escaped her facade and sat back in her chair and summoned Nora.

"Yes?" she said stepping from shadow.

"I need you to find a body for me."

"You didn't convert it?" asked Nora surprised. Luciana always converted bodies, not matter how distracted she got.

"I neglected to notice it's usefulness."

"Where is the is the body?"

"Somewhere around the palace."

Nora's eyes widened. "Who is it you want me to find."

Luciana looked at her devilishly. "Princess Selene's little brother.

Chapter Sixteen

S elene was running, towards the voice of her little brother. She could hear him calling her, his little innocent voice. She could hear him, she knew she was getting closer and closer and then there he was, only it wasn't him.

"Albin?" The little boy turned around and she looked at him more closely. It was her little brother, only his appearance had changed. His clothes were no longer gold and white, they were silver and black,

"Who are you?"

"I–I'm your sister."

"Mommy!" He clutched onto a woman draped in black and Selene became sick. Luciana looked at her vixenishly and knelt down to sooth Albin who was crying.

"Aw, hush baby, don't worry," she said not taking her eyes off Selene.

"Mommy, who is she? She scares me."

"Aw, she shouldn't, she's just one of the bad people that want's to kill me."

"No! He hugged her and sent Selene sprawling back with a wave of his hand. "You won't kill my mommy!"

Selene jerked awake, and tried to gain control of her breathing. She wiped her forehead and looked down at Edel who was sound asleep. She crept out of bed and went to get some fresh air.

Selene walked outside and stopped short as Líead was standing by a tree.

"Líead?" Líead turned around and stared at her with understanding eyes.

"Selene, what's wrong?"

"Nightmare, about my little brother. Why are you out here?"

"Couldn't sleep." They just stared at each other before Selene sat down.

"She needs to die Líéad."

"Now hold on Selene, she's already dead. What you mean is that she needs to be destroyed, and although I am in complete agreement with you, killing her out of vengeance is not the way, it isn't right."

"Then what am I suppose to do? I don't know what is right, or what is wrong, and at this point, who cares."

"You're wrong." Líéad sat across form her and took her hands. "Every decision affects us all Selene, all you have to do in life is choose correctly or devastation will take over. A perfect example is now in time."

"But how do I know what is right?"

"I'm going to tell you a story, one the elves would tell to me. There was once a girl, the second cousin to the princesses. Her mother died when she was very young and her father chose to leave and not take care of her. He thought *that* was the right thing to do, leaving her with her people instead if taking her with him. Now, her heart was shattered, making her prone to sickness, even though her body was strong. Her father would write every so often and he would come back to visit.

"This girl became a Ranger and very beautiful. There was a man who asked for her hand in marriage. Unfortunately is wasn't looked kindly on when an elf took a hand without her fathers approval. So she ran home and asked for the latest latter from her father. Her aunts stared at her sadly, and with that glance she knew that there was no letter, he hadn't sent one. So the girl ran off into the night and met a group of travellers bent in destroying the Dark Lord. So she chose to join, to prove her worth so that she could get married. That was the right choice because it helped, it didn't destroy. But something happened, do you know what?"

"No."

"She was killed. Do you know who she was, who she is?"

"Who?"

"General Entia. Had her father stayed or taken her with him, she would not be what she is now. Do you understand Selene?"

Selene stared at her and noticed a bit of passion, a bit of anger in her eyes. "Yes."

"Good, just think about why you want to kill her, you need to make the right choice Selene, or the outcome could be disastrous."

"I understand. But Líéad do you think it was hard for her father, making a choice?"

Líead's eyes grew cold and dark. "He shouldn't have been given a choice, he should have taken care of her." She stood up and lifted Selene to her feet. "You should go to bed Selene, you're going to need it."

"You're right, I should. I'll see you tomorrow." Selene walked back to her room and stopped briefly at her mirror. She felt odd, she looked a bit odd, if only she knew why.

*   *   *

Entia stared up at Selene's just to make sure that the damn girl was fast asleep.

"That was very sentimental," said a voice.

Entia turned around to see Luciana behind her, a glass of wine glowing blood red in her porcelain hands. Her eyes glowing jade.

"I try. She's pathetic, easy to toy with. Her emotions are so—"

"Predictable?" offered Luciana.

"Exactly. She is so pathetic, besides this story will make her more likely to defeat, her pity will over come her. It's only matter of time."

"You are just so brilliant."

"Thank you. Now what was she ranting about?"

Luciana smiled. "Oh just a little glimpse into the future. I'm sending Nathaniel and Nora to go find his body. I'm going to restore it. Just a little twist into my already brilliant plan." She smiled malevolently and drank a bit of wine before offering some to Entia who took a long deserved sip.

"Thank you, all they have is ale. I think it's beginning to make me sick," she joked and Luciana laughed, The knew it wasn't the ale, but her fathers presence

"Entia, I have a question, why do you think that she gave him most of *her* power to Donovan and not to Bella or Trixie or Coryn or even Corbett?"

"Because all though history a father should have a strong loving bond with his children, they are suppose to be protectors." Entia clenched her fist and crushed the glass.

"Oh dear," said Luciana mockingly. She waved her hand and the glass was one again. Entia's hand though was not.

"It's not healing."

"I'm glad you noticed," said Luciana hotly. She took her hand and examined the cuts. She slapped Entia on her head and healed her hand.

"Thank you."

"Make sure Donovan, or anyone for that matter does not sense this, if they do—"

"I know, I'll be careful."

Luciana left her alone and Entia noticed the wine was still there. She grabbed it and drank it down. If she was going to survive these retched people, she would need it.

*   *   *

Luciana was practicing her swordsmanship with his majesty. Her armour barely covered her but then again it didn't serve a point, a sword usually had a tendency to go through armour when used with enough force, which Corbett was sure to use.

"So the child?" inquired the Dark Lord as he aimed for her head..

"Plan B, just in case I don't manage to bear a child," she said shoving it back.

"Hmm, well then, I must say I am impresses."

"You weren't before?" She parried off a hit next to her heart.

"Well, to be honest, I only wanted to possess you because you had immense power, I hoped that would be enough, but your intelligence and agile hatred is most astounding."

Her eyes widened in realization.

"You were watching me?"

"There were whispers, so I began to sense and I began to watch, hence why I took you." Luciana smiled and disarmed him easily. She would have loved to killed him again, if it weren't for the fact that she had already done it once.

"I must say, I am glad I surprise you . . . Bartholomew."

"How dare you—"

She waved the sword near his face. "Yes I know, I called you by your true name. I believe I have earned that right have I not." Her voice was cold. She had killed him once and she would do it again, and enjoy it even more.

He smiled. "I can feel your hatred *Luci*. It does serve you, greatly, something I find very admirable."

"You're a bastard." She sheathed her sword and grabbed him and shoved him back into the mirror. He stood by it, still gleaming in his youth. His black coal eyes burned with an intensity toward her that made her wonder.

"Go ahead ask."

"Why me and not my sister? She is after all more destructive in her use of magic."

He chuckled. "You had control over it though. You also have a charm that she lacks, that they all lack. I must say, I was even . . . infatuated with you. I loved your power more though."

"Hmm," remarked Luciana as she stood still staring at him. A door opened and in walked Nora.

"Luciana, we found the body. In walked Nathaniel carrying a childlike body. "His body is severely deteriorated—"

"Bring him in and lay him on the ground. I don't care how badly deteriorated it is." Luciana was a bit upset. The dark lord was a bastard.

Nora took the body from Nathaniel and laid in on the ground. Seven years had not been good to the little boy.

Luciana watched as Nora and Nathaniel left and locked the door behind them. She knelt down to the boy and cupped his little face.

"You are going to be brilliant young one." A dark light spread form the hands and covered the body in a blanket. The room glowed a dark purple and slowly began to burn out. This was taking more strength than she had, she thought. Finally, with a great force of power, the boy was finished. She dug into Selene's memories, hoping to find the name of the boy and with luck she did. She smiled and knelt down to the little one's ear.

"Time to wake up, Albin." She watched as his eyes fluttered open and looked up at her.

"Who are you?"

Luciana faked a false impression of worry. "Well I'm you mother. Did that evil witch erase your memory? Can you tell me your names? Can you remember?" He shook his head.

"No, I can't. Mom, who am it?" He sat up and looked at her. Luciana cupped his face and smiled.

"You are Albin, my son, protector of your little brother, the heir to the throne. You are the prince of Knights."

"I am?"

"Uh huh, and this is your grandfather." She stood up and grabbed his hand. Luciana lead him to the mirror and there appeared Bartholomew, with and eerie warm smile on his face.

"Hello grandson." The young boy put his hand on the glass and Luciana wrapped her arms around him, like a mother should.

"Albin, would you like to meet your many aunts and uncles?" He looked at her, a wide smiled brightly lit on his face and suddenly all nine generals appeared from the darkness and smiled at him.

Chapter Seventeen

Luciana had patience, especially for her son. She watched as he concentrated hard on the candle. He was going to light it, or so she hoped, for if he couldn't, then he was useless to her because beyond fighting, he needed to know magic. Suddenly as she contemplated what to do should he fail, the candle burst to life. Luciana smiled and clapped for her son. He sat back, exhausted. He was older, but then again he had been dead seven years and the body, being revived had to compensate for it. He wasn't five anymore, he was twelve and it was taking his mind a bit longer to catch up.

He kept his gaze towards the ground as she clapped and she knew exactly what to say.

"Albin look at me." He did and she smiled warmly, "you did good Albin, really, that was wonderful."

"It took me too long. I need to practice more." Luciana smiled and cupped his face.

"Don't worry Albin, it took me a long time to master spells as well, it's okay. Once you've got a handle on it, it all moves rather quickly, besides your swordsmanship it spectacular, and that took you almost a month——"

"But that wasn't as exhausting mother, I could practice for hours, but this—" he gestured to the candle and it went out, "it takes too much."

Luciana gleamed. "Did it take you much to put it out?"

Albin stared at her then at the candle. "Well no, not really—"

"And why is that, do you think?"

"'Cause I already know how the magic worked around it."

"Exactly, you already knew, so with practice, you will learn more. Now come, you seem exhausted, lets get some food in you my young general." He beamed and stood up and waited for his mother like any good son.

"Mum, when do I get a horse and my own fleet?"

Luciana smiled at his anxiousness. He was brilliant and would have made a fine king, had she not come into the picture. "Soon Albin, soon."

"Has it been announced? When will I get to battle them, and that witch who claims to be my sister, the one who wants to kill my little brother and you and everyone."

Luciana laughed and hugged him. He wasn't a waste of magic, in fact he was worth every bit.

"Patience my son, patience."

"Yeah okay." He hugged her and they continued down the stairs.

*   *   *

They were resting, and they needed it, but lately, they could afford it. For some reason, the generals had calmed down. Something was going on and they all knew it, Corbett knew it so staying where they were, was actually a good idea, and it was much needed. Selene hadn't had an invasion, which was good, but it bothered Corbett. Luciana wasn't one to give up, she never was, even before her turn to darkness. He watched Selene laugh with Líead. He was glad that they had found her, she was strong and a good friend to Selene. He had to admit there was something familiar about the way she walked as well as her coughing spasms. Líead must have noticed him because she turned to him and smiled warmly. He smiled back and she turned back to Selene who was eating an apple form the many apple trees.

"Corbett—" He turned his head at the sudden sound of his name. Luciana was whispering for him. He couldn't go to her, he shouldn't, but that voice, that beautiful joyful voice was not that of the Dark Empress, it was his Luci.

"Corbett . . . lets play." Her voice giggle and he smiled despite himself.

He walked away and no one followed. It was normal. He walked down to the nearby stream and sitting there was Luciana with her feet in the water laughed and smiling. He took a step and felt himself pass a barrier. He stopped and Luciana looked up at him smiling.

"So they can't see you, or find you."

He said nothing but continued to look at her, then finally resumed his walk towards her.

"You're not speaking to me?" She stood up and took a step into the stream and stared at him. Her ignored her question and stepped into the water.

"Hello Luci," he said finally as he smiled.

She smiled back happily. "Hello Corbett."

Corbett finally kissed her and she kissed him back. This was his Luci, the girl he loved, the one he was going to marry. He picked her up and Luciana giggled in joy which caused him to laugh.

Back on land Corbett held her close and kissed her tenderly. He missed kissing her like this, he missed her period.

"Corbett—"

"Luciana—" He pulled away and looked at her kind and gentle face. She smiled up at him and stroked his face.

"Shh, my love." She kissed him and Corbett found that he could not stop himself. This was *his* Luciana, his Luci.

"Oh how pathetic," came a voice. That was her voice, Lucianas voice, the Dark Empress. Corbett sat up and looked down at the Luci in his arms who was now fierce and ready to fight. She jerked up and Corbett followed as she pulled out her sword. He looked at what she was staring at, it was Luciana, clad in black, the completely opposite of his Luci.

"Oh Corbett, having fun?" She laughed a cold hateful laugh.

"Ignore her Corbett, just going I can take care of her." He looked back and forth between them and didn't know what to make of any of it.

"Oh yes Corbett, go, run, skip walk, you're so good at that I really must say." She laughed again and pulled out her sword. "Well what are you two waiting for, come and get me."

Luci charged and Luciana blocked her. Corbett watched as they fought and saw Luciana summoning a second sword. Corbett ran and blocked her from attacking his Luci.

"Oo, my my Corbett, how very brave of you. Now just sit back down and watch." She knocked him to the ground and kicked him in his gut as he fell. By the time he lifted his head he was too late. Luciana had both of her swords thrust through Luci. He sat there awestruck and watched as she fell to the ground, her sword echoing after her. Corbett screamed and ran to her.

"Luci, no, you can't, not again, I can't lose you again." Tears fell on her face and Luci cupped her face.

"Oh Corbett, you aren't losing me again . . . you already lost me, so very long ago." Her eyes fluttered close and her head fell back. Corbett laid her down and sat there crying.

"Poor little pathetic Corbett," said Luciana as she circled away from him. "What's wrong? Lose someone you love . . . again." She laughed and it echoed all around.

"Evil witch!"

She jerked her head back at him, a disfiguring snarl on her face.

"You're calling me evil!? You are the one responsible for turning me into this!! You left me to die! That girl, this girl," she said bending down and grabbing Luci's face. "This girl died in a dungeon the moment she knew she would have to escape on her own and she stayed dead when she saw you kiss that stupid Princess! You killed her Corbett, not the Darkness." Luciana threw Lucis' face the ground and stood up. "You killed me Corbett, three times: when you abandoned me, when you betrayed me, and when you left me. You never even once tried to save me."

Luciana turned and walked off. "Go back to your friends Corbett, to your princess. Enjoy the time you have, the only time you'll have."

Corbett looked around and noticed that he was alone and that the sky had changed. It was dusk.

"Did you kill her, or attempt it," came a voice. He jerked up and around and found himself face to face with Trixie and Donovan. Corbett picked up his sword walked past them.

"I already killed her . . . a long time ago," he said sheathing his sword violently.

*   *   *

Selene was laughing along with Líead. They had so much in common, it was as though she knew her. Selene picked up another cooked fish and handed another one to Líead who waved it off. Líead was telling the few jokes she knew, the only ones that existed considering the elf folk.

"Okay another. Hmm . . . okay, why are Rangers scared of their shadows?"

"Why?"

"Because they can't tell who is friends and who is foe!" Selene laughed, not because the jokes where funny but because it proved that the elves were mortal and had senses of humour like humans.

"Enough jokes," said Cade suddenly.

They both looked at Cade and watched as he walked off. Líead grumbled under her breath and picked up her fish right off the fire and bit into it.

"Líéad! Are you all right?" exclaimed Selene staring at her hand.

"I'm fine, why?"

"You grabbed that right off the fire, how are you–"

"Don't ask, but to put it simply, I'm pretty much immune to pain." She didn't smile and leaned against a tree as she ate her fish. Selene noticed that Cade was staring at Líéad and walked away when he met Selene's glance. "Líéad what do you make of that outburst?"

"I'm mocking the elves, his kind and he knows it, and to top it off, he doesn't blame me."

"Oh."

They sat there in silence and Líéad picked up a fallen apple.

"I'm going to go talk to him alone, I feel . . . I don't know confused."

"Why?"

"I had a fiancé. He was an elf, but he died along with everyone in the village. He was hoping I at least would escape, but no, my love died in vain." She stopped up and began to walk away but Selene, stopped her.

"Wait, Líéad, what was his name?"

She smiled warmly. "Silkas."

Trixie's ears twitched and she looked at Líéad.

"What did you say?"

"My fiancé, his name is . . . was Silkas."

"Huh–" Trixie muttered something in audible and bit her lip.

"Is something wrong?"

Trixie looked back at her, secretively, and shook her head. "No."

"Okay then." Líéad grinned briefly then walked off after Cade. Trixie remained there sensing the air around her. There was nothing malignant about Líéad, nothing at all. She walked off to Donovan who was bracing a saddle on a horse. He did not look up to meet her presence.

"Donovan, I need to speak with you for a moment."

"About?"

"Líéad, her fiancé was named Silkas—"

"Silkas died in battle Trixie, I killed him remember." He finally stopped and looked at her. "It just another reason they both hate me. It's common name Trixie–"

She shook her head and stared at him. "It *was* a common name Donovan. Look it just feels, I don't know, out of place. I can't explain it Donovan."

"Relax, everything is all right."

"No it's not Donovan. I feel *it* in the air, in the Earth."

Donovan took her by the shoulders and looked deep into her eyes.

"That is because of Luciana and her spreading darkness. That is because of what we have done."

She stared deeply into his eyes, and knew that he was probably right, but she felt something off in te air, something not right.

"If you're sure."

"I am, now go on, relax."

Trixie nodded and looked at Líead who was very close to Cade. She smiled slightly then looked at Selene who was staring at Edel.

*   *   *

Luciana watched Selene though the crystal ball. The one she stole from Nora, the one she used against Nora. The princess just sat there. She shifted around looking for Corbett but couldn't find him. She ended the feeble spell and sat there in her throne for but a moment, thinking.

Albins' mind had finally caught up with his body. She decided she would check up on her son.

In the courtyard, ten men from every general including each of the eight generals were fighting against Albin and losing. He had undying strength for battle. She summoned her own sword and decided to enter the battle. She struck form behind but he sensed her blocked her. He wasn't going to let his emotions deter him, a good sign. He blocked her and summoned another sword to parry off Nora. He rolled away, quickly then threw daggers like Damien taught him, grabbing his hidden ones from his boots and hit Nora in her neck. She fell to the ground and stayed there. Next Esmerelda and Adira sent arrows flying but he shot them ack at them. He beat them all, only Luciana was left and he was ready to strike. Luciana threw down her sword and applauded.

"Brilliant, simply brilliant, really my son. You are ready now, to become my tenth general. All we need now is a symbol for you don't you agree?"

"You really think I'm ready?" She nodded and he instantly dropped his swords and ran to her, embracing her. "I love you mother."

Luciana was taken back, but nonetheless happy. She didn't need Corbett to have a family, she already had a beautifully dark one. She hugged him back and looked at Nora, who's neck wounds were healing nicely.

"Nora do you have any ideas?"

"How bout the royal symbol with an A over it." She smiled and hugged him.

"Albin step back for a moment." She placed her hand on Albin chest and a black light enveloped him. His armour change and when the light faded, his armour was new with the symbol placed on it.

"Albin, gather your men, a handful, the same with you Nora and you Damien. I want you to head for the town of Taylen. Our old friends are going there and I want them to meet our new general." Luciana walked back to her castle and touched the jewel in her hand. She would destroy them, inside and out.

Chapter Eighteen

Selene sat on her horse. They were only a day away from the town of Taylen. She missed beds with blankets and cushions and warmth. She smiled at the though but her day dream was quickly shattered when she felt someone punch her shoulder. She turned and saw Líead smiling at her.

"Stop daydreaming Selene, you're drooling and I don't want you to fall off that horse, you need to be fit for the battle to come!" She laughed and Selene joined her.

"You're right Líead, thank you." She trailed along and saw Líead pull her horse closer.

"You weren't daydreaming about Edel were you?"

Selene shook her head. "For once no, I wasn't. Do you often think about Silkas?"

Líead's demeanor changed and her face changed. "Yes. He chose to stand by me, he fought his own people, for me, for my family, to protect us, to love me and he died for ir. I love him still, and the elf who took him from me, I swore revenge against him. I will kill him one day, I must."

"Did you know him? The elf who murdered Silkas?"

She shook her head. "No, he came to trade every so often. I never knew him, not personally anyway."

"I'm sorry."

"Don't be, it's not your fault, you caused nothing." She smiled serenely then turned her attention back to the road. Selene followed suit and they trotted along in silence until they were jerked to a stop. Selene and Líead looked at each other questionably then got off their horses and walked forward to see what was going on.

"Edel," called Selene, "what's going on?"

"I don't know, Arlis?"

"Our elf scout has returned. He said he has news about Luciana."

"Arlis, Edel, Selene come you need to hear this, " called Nila. They looked at each other and Selene looked at Líead who urged her to go on. Selene did so regretfully and upon a return glance saw Líead in the company of Cade.

"What's going on?" asked Galen.

"Empress Luciana has a tenth general."

"What," said Arlis.

"She has a tenth general, a boy the age of twelve. They say that he is her son. He has blonde hair, almost pale as snow and hazel eyes. His symbol though, it is like nothing I would have expected."

"What is it?" asked Selene frightened.

"A skeletal version of *your* royal symbol with the letter A over it."

"What?"

"Nora and Damien travel with him, never leave his side. He calls then Auntie Nora and Uncle Damien. Whoever this new general truly is, his family, we can bet that Luciana made him a general for a reason."

"I suppose we will see him tomorrow," said Selene. The description made her stomach turn. It sounded familiar, it sounded like her little brother. He brother who was murdered, who had looked like their father. She wanted to vomit as her dream flew back to the fore front of her memory.

"Selene," asked Edel.

Selene had not noticed him next to her. "Yes Edel?"

His eyes were full of concern. "Are you all right?"

"Yes, it's just—"

"I know, it does sound like Albin, but Albin was five when he died, she's probably just doing this to both frighten and distract you, don't worry about it okay."

"If you say so." She smiled and he kissed her forehead and walked back to his horse. She walked back to her horse and looked around for Líead who was laughing with Cade. Selene smiled, she was happy that she was happy, that she had already found someone to fill the Void in her heart. Now if only she could win her love and achieve closing the void withing her own heart.

*   *   *

It was the dead of night when they arrived at the town gates of Taylen. Selene got of her horse and walked close to it. *They* knew what she looked like, except the new general, or so she hoped.

They arrived at the inn and paid for room and stalls. Selene sat in a dark corner between Edel and Líead, who were now her formally established guardians, since it was them whom she hung out with the most. Selene looked around and stared at Artemisa who was with Blake, Artemisa simply smiled at her then looked back at Blake. Selene had been neglecting her company for that of Líead and she could see the hurt in her friends eyes. But she couldn't understand, Líead knew her pain, Artemisa did not.

"Selene, I'm going to get something to drink, do you want anything?" asked Líead.

"N-no, thank you."

"If you're sure." She got up and walked over to the bar.

"Selene are you all right?" asked Edel.

She shook her head to answer no. "They all know my face Edel, and this tenth general, he frightens me. The whole idea of it frightens me. Why would she introduce a new general now, after all this time, why not one she stole those six centuries she spent in hiding. What makes this boy so special? It is just so frightening to me so much, I don't know what to think."

Suddenly a pint was placed in front of her face and above it stood Líead.

"Drink Selene, you need to, it'll help you relax. I think even Edel agrees with me, don't you?" She smiled at him and he laughed. Selene looked at him startled and he composed himself.

"Edel you can't—"

"Actually I do Selene. You need to relax."

"But—"

"No buts, we out rule you two to one. Now drink up Selene." With that Líead took her seat and watched Selene. Despite herself Selene smiled at her and began to drink but stopped stricken at the sight of General Nora. Her cape flapped behind her elegantly behind her as she walked into the tavern.

She was outside her body. She did not realize she was being shoved under the table by Líead and Edel. She knew she was but couldn't not, was nat aware of anything happening. Finally her senses returned to her.

"Lí—"

"Shut up Selene," she said ruthlessly. "She's looking for you. Just stay down."

"But–"

"Hush Selene," said Edel.

Selene looked at him but yielded nonetheless. She sat there for a minute till she heard the door open once again.

"Nora, have you found anything?"

"No Damien, if I did you would see a neck in my hand." She looked at him arrogantly. "But I feel something. White magic, and it's strong here. They are here, as Luciana said."

"Her son, what do we do, he's getting restless, and he keeps beating me up." He laughed and leaned against the door. "It's amusing, but my body is beginning to ache somewhat."

"Hmph," then under her breath, "someone I know is here."

"What was that Nora?"

She shook her head. "Nothing, lets get back to the boy, he'll need us around. I'm sure they know about him by now."

"Probably, but do they know his identity." He laughed and walked toward her.

"Oh Damien, you are so very amusing, now come." She walked out and he followed her out.

When the door shut, Selene felt Líead grab her arm and lift her from under the table.

"Are you okay?"

"No."

"Okay." She looked at the door. "I wonder who this new general is, and why is he so significant."

"We'll find out soon enough. Líead take her up to her room." She nodded and did just that, helping her stand and walk.

Once again outside herself, Selene kept thinking about her dream. Albin had called her an evil witch, had used powerful magic *against* had, and called Luciana mother. The question haunted her endlessly: What if the new general was her brother?

She was not aware when Líead left her, only aware of the far away words she left behind telling her that she would be in her room if needed. Selene thinks she smiled, to sooth the worry that had been on Líead's face. She hoped that for one night, she would need no one, no matter how much she might cry.

A sound brought her back to reality and she was finally aware of how alone she was when Líead had closed the door. A bright smiled sprung onto her face and she was thankful for Líead. She seemed to care most of all in these dire days.

*   *   *

Entia locked the door behind her as she entered her room. She didn't need people looking for her, needing to talk to her as she tried to rest.

"How's my favourite elf," came a voice. Entia smiled and looked at Damien.

"I was just coming to see you." He held out his hand to her and smiled. She took it smiling and was suddenly in Albins room.

"Auntie Entia!" He came and hugged her and she hugged him back.

"So how is my favourite general," said Entia.

"And here I though I was your favourite," said Damien, feigning sadness.

"You flatter yourself too much Damien," remarked Nora as she sharpened her sword.

"Auntie Entia, when are you going to get rid of this disguise?"

"Soon Albin, when your mother sees fit that I should. I'm sure it will be when we reach the tavern by the fortress."

"Good, I hate seeing you as thus, I like you're true appearance far better." Entia smiled. "As do I."

"So what news," asked Nora putting her sword down.

"The princess is scared, she thinks it's—" Entia stopped briefly and looked at Albin. Luciana would murder her is she messed up this far into the plan. "She thinks it is you."

He stared at her disgusted. "Her brother? I am not her brother, she tried to kill me. I have but one sibling, the future ruler of Radiencia! Evil witch! I'll kill her, I swear I will!"

"Good Albin." Entia smiled, Luciana was brilliant. "So I hear that you are beating up Damien, is it as much fun as it sound?" They all laughed except Damien who glared at them.

"Oh Damien, we are only joking," said Nora.

"Whatever, you are lucky that we fight on the same side."

Nora laughed. "Oh, I'm the lucky one?! Damien have you forgotten that I always defeat you."

Albin and Entia laughed even harder and Damien glared at them then turned back to Nora. In all her arrogance, she was stunning.

"Ah, I miss this," said Entia distracting him. "Now, they are headed toward Isabelle, we know that. They don't really have a plan, all they know, or think is that Corbett has to kill Luciana, and no one else."

"Pathetic fools, no one can kill her," said Albin hotly.

Entia shared the same worried look with Damien and Nora bore on their faces. They were becoming mortal and there was one way, but one way to end her life, that luckily they had not figured, that all their lives depended on them not figuring out.

"Hmm, I had better go," she said distracted. "That pathetic princess may wake up from another nightmare." She laughed and snapped her fingers quickly

Back in her room she laid on the bed. Albin did not know, he could never know she assumed. And Corbett, he could never figure it out. She stared at the ceiling and thought of what would ever happen. Would everything be as it once was? Would she be able to go home? Would she find a new love? Could she ever be happy with her father?

She sat up and looked at the mirror and her joy of tricking returned to her, as well as her anger and hatred towards all. She was having fun, especially when she noticed the rip between her father and Trixie. Silkas name and caused a disturbance. She closed her eyes in remembrance. Silkas, her love, killed by her father.

So he had came after her, to help and protect her and Luciana had welcomed her with open arms giving her power. Entia had welcomed death, and her love had stayed by her side, turned on them all, just to be by her side. But then he, the man who called himself her father had placed an arrow deep into his heart, and she did not have the power to reach him, didn't know how to save him as she held him dying, didn't know the power she had contained.

Entia clenched her fist and wept. She had love Silkas with all her heart, and would always. He had given up everything just for her.

A knock shook her and she wiped the tears off her cheeks and took a deep breath before opened her door. Cade stood before her and she froze.

"Líead," he said seeing the tears in her eyes, "are you all right?"

She shook her head. "No, not really."

"Do you want to talk about it? Can I come in?"

She smiled tenderly. "Yes, of course." He smiled at her and she closed the door, a mischievous glint in her cold violet eyes.

*　　*　　*

Corbett stood alone just outside the town. Who was this new tenth general that was Luciana's son. He knew that it wasn't truly hers. He wondered who this boy was and thought that maybe, just maybe it was Albin, it was the only plausible conclusion, and he knew Luciana's mind inside and out, unfortunately.

"Oh what's wrong my love, scared," laughed Luciana. She was before him, crawling out from the trunk of a willow tree. She stayed far from him and kept her eyes on his. Her gaze penetrated her, bothered her, because of all he knew. It ached him to see her.

"Go away," he said looking up at the sky.

"Oh what's wrong? Don't tell me my son has already killed someone, and here I though I told him to behave." She laughed venomously. She would always be able to find him, he could never hide from her, no matter how much he tried. They were bonded, felt each others joy and heartache, the would never be able to escape each other, no matter how much either of them tried.

"Who is it?" he asked bluntly finally looked at her.

"As if I would tell you. Please Corbett, give me more credit then that."

"Luci—" She shot him a cold tormented glance.

"Don't call me that, I am not *your* Luci, no longer in any case." She smiled. "But please, what do you want, humour me." Her face was impassive but Corbett could see her mind at work.

"Who is it?"

Luciana rolled her eyes. "I already said I would not tell you, why would you ask again." Her eye turned back to their jade hue. "Now, what were you really going to say?" She walked up to him and looked deep into his eyes. He wanted to ask her to run away with him, as he has done before, but instead he grabbed her and kissed her. She pulled away calmly and looked at him tenderly. Her eyes were beginning to water and Corbett could not fathom why.

"Now I am your Luci." She kissed him for but a minute then was gone and he was left alone. Something though, was left in his hand. He looked down and saw that it was his necklace, the one he had give to her when he had asked her to marry him. He clutched jade stone tightly. It had belonged to his parents and after their death he had kept it to remember why he was doing what he had planned, why he had set out on the quest that would most likely end in death.

Corbett had given it to her out of love because he loved her, and it had matched her eyes so perfectly. His Luci had given it back to him to remind him of everything. He clutched it and wept as he did so.

Luciana stood at her window looking over the terrain. Tears fell down her cheek as she clutched her shattered heart. She would make him pay, she would make them all pay and shatter all their hearts one by one.

"Luciana—" came Corbett's voice.

"Corbett—" returned Luciana's.

They both looked up at the dark night sky remembering their love, remembering their hatred, remembering their promises to each other and then soon slept in their darkness, alone.

Chapter Nineteen

Corbett stood alongside Coryn, Donovan, Trixie and Selene. He looked at her and then back at Coryn who was glaring at him. He had to control his emotions like Coryn had said.

They needed food for the rest of their trip that was sure to take a while.

"So, what are we going to do, just stand here?" asked Selene annoyed. She was sick of being locked up.

"We need to think Selene," said Trixie faintly agitated. "They know what you look like therefore we need to watch them. And do not to forget the new general, we don't know what he looks like, we need to find him."

"What if *I* don't want to?"

"Then go back to your room," said Trixie hotly as he glared at her. Trixie was sick of her being a child. She knew nothing of could happen.

"I've been there for three days straight, I'm sick off it."

"I'll take care of her," said a voice. Corbett turned around and looked at Líead who stared back at him sweetly. "I'll take her and look around, don't worry, I'll make sure she stays safe."

"I don't—" began Trixie.

"Okay, but be careful," said Corbett glaring at Trixie.

Líeadbowed her head slightly. "Thank you." Líead grabbed Selene and dragged her down the road.

When they were far enough out of ear shot Corbett began to yell at Trixie. "Trixie, what the hell was that?"

"She doesn't care about her safety Corbett! We are risking our lives to make sure she becomes queen, the first true queen in seven years, of Radiencia, and she, she couldn't care less about anything!"

"Give it a rest," said Donovan suddenly. "Luciana is torturing her, invading her mind day in and day out, invading her personal thoughts. Luciana wants her alive or dead, she has a specific plan for her."

"She needs to care more though Donovan. More about what we are risking."

"Enough Trixie," said Donovan and Corbett in unison.

"You think she doesn't realize that Trixie, she does, you know she does," continued Corbett.

"Not—"

Corbett waved his hand to shut her up. "Just enough, I don't want yo hear anymore just go buy some food okay." Corbett turned and walked away, headed the other way followed close by Donovan.

"What do you think is really bothering her?"

"Damien. Seeing him, hearing him, it bothers her considering he was the one that shot her with that poisonous arrow."

"Hmm, Corbett do you think any of us are going to die? I mean she almost did?"

"When considering that fact, we may, after all we are becoming mortal once again. Death is always a possibility."

"Do you think Luciana *can* be killed?"

He shrugged. "There may be a way."

"Do you think Adiras' and Entias' lives are tied to her."

"They're dead Donovan, Luciana is not. She gave herself away while she was alive. Nathaniel was near death, Nora, all of them had no way of living without the dark magic. If she dies, they all die."

"I though as much. I was just hoping that maybe I could save my daughter and my love."

"Even if you could, they would still hate you, you killed Silkas."

"He betrayed us."

"No he didn't. He stayed alongside Entia, he stayed true to his heart, he chose to remain faithful to his heart. He may have betrayed us, but we would learn a thing or two from him."

Corbett left Donovan and touched the pendant in his pocket. He should have stayed true to his heart, maybe if he had, he'd be resting with Luciana.

Corbett kept walking till finally he stopped at a place. Right now he needed to think about supplies, not the past.

"Can I help you?"

"I hope so—"

"How mush is this sword?" came a cold child-like voice. Corbett turned his head slightly and his eyes widened as he stared at Nora and the tenth general.

*   *   *

Selene and Líead made their way around admiring all the things they wished they could buy but couldn't. She wondered where Edel was at the moment. She missed him, but then again it was her fault, she was being distant, immersed deep within her thought of the tenth general and his identity.

"Selene are you all right?"

"No not really. I'm a fugitive princess, hiding on the run, for my life, and people are risking their lives so that I live and take control and be queen. Líead I don't think I want to be the queen of all Radiencia, it's just too much, it really is. I was never groomed for it. Me and my sister we were groomed to be the mage's of the king, our little brother. He was always so sick, so frail at times, but I knew that he would grow up to be a brilliant king."

"What are you getting at?"

Selene stared at her worried, her face contorted in it. "Líead, Luciana is merciless, I think that the tenth general may be my brother."

"But he's twelve, wasn't your brother five when he died, and why would she bring your sister back as well and have two generals against you."

"I don't know, I'm just so confused."

"Come on lets keep walking and enjoy the day." Líead smiled and Selene did the same and they walked arm in arm together down the street. Selene couldn't help but wonder why she had been so hostile when she first met her, there was nothing dark about her. Suddenly, Líead pulled Selene into and alley and placed her hand over her mouth.

"Líead?"

"Shh, General Nora just got out of a store with who I suspect to be the tenth general."

Selene shut up and sunk to the ground behind some barrels. Líead leaned against the wall casually as though she had nothing to hide and pretended to stare blankly into space.

Selene peeked from behind the barrels and waited.

"You have a sword, why do you want this one," said General Nora.

"Because Auntie Nora, I wanted to do her a favour and take away any opportunity that people want for rebellion, they do not need a sword, there is no need."

Selene knew that voice and couldn't help but stand up. Her eyes widened and Líead stared at her.

"Selene?"

"Oh my god . . . that's my brother!" She feel down in tears and she stared at the body, the older body of her dead brother.

*   *   *

Entia did not think Selene would still be conscious or would react the way she did. Actually she was hoping that she would have fallen unconscious so that everything could be easier to explain.

She helped the pathetic princess walk back to the inn where they were staying. She looked around for a familiar face form the past and finally found one.

"Cor—Arlis! Arlis!" He looked at her then at the frail frightened figure of Selene and ran over.

"Líead what happened?"

"She saw the tenth general and it is her brother. Apparently Luciana did some kind of magic I don't know, but she's in shock."

"Selene talk to me, please breath, I need you to breath. Please talk and tell me what happened exactly." He cupped her face and Entia noticed that Selene couldn't and more importantly wouldn't. She wanted to deny the truth, hide from it. As she continued to do was shake her head.

"Líead?"

"I saw Nora, I dragged her into an alley and hid her but her curiosity got the better of her and well she had to see who te tenth general was. All she's been doing is mumbling, denying what she saw."

All of a sudden Selene stood up and went up to her, pointing at the door. "THAT THING IS NOT MY BROTHER! THAT IS AN ABOMINATION!"

"Selene—" began Entia frightened.

"NO! THAT IS NOT MY BROTHER! HE DIED AT THE HANDS OF THE WOMAN HE CALLS MOTHER!" She watched Selene fall to the ground in tears. People were staring all around at her. Entia didn't know what to do.

"Líead, take her to her room."

She nodded. "Yeah, okay."

Entia picked her up and tried with all her might to bring Selene to her room. When she was angry, she was powerful and finally she knew why Luciana had sent her here, why she had risen the body of Selene's brother and not her sister. She laid Selene down and left her to be in her room and stormed into her room and locked the door.

"Luciana!" she screamed as she stormed into her room, vanishing quickly into Luciana's. Luciana lay on her bed.

"What?"

"You really think it!"

"Thank what?"

"You think you're going to die?"

"No . . . I know I am Entia. It's the only way."

"Only way for what?"

"For the darkness to thrive. Corbett will kill me in anger and I will then be able to possess that princess. All part of my plan."

"So I've finally noticed," she said crossing her arms. "You're attracted to her power, as well as the fact that she's so easy to manipulate and that she's their last hope."

Luciana stood up and glared at her. "*His* last hope. Who cares about anyone else, he is their leader."

Entia bowed her head in forgiveness. "Of course. So you've told no one, not even Nathaniel?"

"No one, I have to die, you all will live but I will have to die to take over Selene's body. I will live through her, in her."

"You are quick on your feet Luciana." She turned around and walked to the door but stopped short. "You always have been."

"I know."

Entia left back to her room and stood there staring at her false refection and waited for Cade to arrive. Then suddenly she had one last thought that she had to comment on.

"Luciana?"

"Yes?"

"I noticed that you didn't have your pendant–"

"I got rid of it!" she hissed and her voice was gone. Entia simply smiled. So that was why Corbett's hand had a home in his pocket.

Chapter Twenty

Luciana reached for her neck once again forgetting that she no longer had her pendant. She swore under her breath.

"Forget again Luci," said two voices. She turned around and stared at Lucas and Jason who's only difference were their eyes.

"Lucas, Jason. How are my oldest friends?"

"Fine," they said and sat down at the foot of her bed.

"Yes?"

"Well our products are selling but nothing gets past Isabelle. She set up a magical barrier to purify the food after the elven incident. She's a quick one," said Lucas.

"Ah, but Luci's quicker, aren't you Luci," said Jason.

Luciana smiled. "Much quicker." She tapped her fingers against her chin and stared deep into space. "A barrier huh, lets go see shall we." She snapped her fingers and walked along the rode with Lucas and Jason trailing behind her from shadows.

"God I hate Light magic," said Lucas.

"Dark magic is much more useful," finished Jason.

"Time to do your magic boys." They laughed and Jason summoned his scythe and flew it into the ground. Lucas summoned his hammer and swords and stabbed his sword into the trees spreading a darkness with his hammer.

"Now, time for me to conceal." Luciana spread her arms and a wave of magic emanated from her and hid the spreading poison.

"Now what," asked Jason and Lucas in unison.

"Now we pay a visit to my dear little sister." Jason and Lucas laughed and followed her as she walked down the dark dirt road. They approached the tavern and Luciana walked in ignoring the closed sign. She stopped at the sight of her younger sister in the arms of another man.

"My, my Bella, I see you fare well." She took a seat and watched as they separated. Isabelle's eyes flared.

"I said get out! What does it take—"

"Oh hush little sister I've had enough of your mouth. Now, what a nice little spell you put up, just thought I would let you know how much your magic has improved. I would be proud of you, if *it* had not cost me dearly." She said harshly embedding her nails into the wood table.

"You?! How 'bout the hundreds of lives you punish daily."

"I wouldn't be punishing them if you had come back to at least check if I was alive! I was your sister Isabelle! You forsake me for selfish reasons. This is all your fault so do not complain to me, look in a mirror . . . if you can face it."

"GET OUT!"

Luciana smiled and got up and began to leave when a thought occurred to her.

"Isabelle, why didn't you ever tell me that Nathaniel we so wonderful in bed?" Isabelle threw a glass at her but she dodged it and watched it shatter against the wall.

"*GET OUT!!*"

"As you wish . . . little sister dear." Luciana vanished in a cloud of black mist an laughed her way to her bedroom followed by Lucas and Jason.

"Luciana that was—"

"Brilliant," finished Jason.

"I know." Seeing Isabelle throw things brought her mind back to Corbett. She looked at Lucas and Jason. "Can you two leave a moment, please, I just remembered something."

"Of course," said Jason.

"Okay," said Lucas. They left the room and Luciana closed her eyes.

A rock hit her window and Isabelle and Luciana jolted awake and looked at each other. They knew who it was. Luciana got out of bed and opened her window, there stood Corbett kicking at the ground.

"Is he okay," asked Isabelle yawning.

Luciana shook her head. "Don't wait up for me okay," Isabelle nodded and Luciana crawling out of his window and jumped down landing in front of Corbett. He looked at her slowly up and down then turned away.

"You didn't get dressed?"

"I never do when you're upset." She suddenly felt very uncomfortable and pulled her shorts down a little. Why did he have to notice her now. Corbett could feel she was uncomfortable but he couldn't help but notice *her*.

"Corbett, do you want to talk about it?"

"No.," he said finally looked away.

"Then what do you want?"

"To just run away! Dammit I just want to leave."

"Okay . . . so why come get me?"

"Because I was hoping you'd run away with me." He looked at her and she smiled and walked over to him, wrapping her arms around his neck. He stared down at her.

"Corbett of course I will run away with you. What are best friends for."

He smiled down at her and wrapped his arms around her.

"Where should we go. I've got the money," he said smiling mischievously.

"Okay, my choice, hmm, we could fo back to the Thieves City, the King of Thieves did love how we did what we do. A mage and a thief." She laugh and he gripped her even tighter.

"Luci–"

"Yes?" looking at him hopefully.

"Thank you."

"For what?"

"Being there when I needed you." He pulled her alongside him as he headed back for his house. In his room he kissed her lightly as always and hugged her close to him as he fell asleep.

*   *   *

Corbett woke in a cold sweat. His stupid childhood memories kept coming back to him every night now. She had always been there for him, but when she needed him the most, he had forgotten her, abandoned her. He got out of bed and put on his pants and buckled up his sword.

The cool night air relaxed and refreshed him so he decide to walk to the city well. It was tranquil there and some water could help clear his mind.

As he approached th well though, he saw a girl sitting there with bright black hair and instantly he knew who it was. It was Líead. She sat on the well and stared up at the sky. He saw her ears twitch like and elf and she looked at him calmly.

"Lose something?"

He smiled. "Not today, just needed a break."

"Life doesn't give breaks, you should know that."

"It's nice to imagine though. So, did you lose something?"

She smiled. "Not today."

"So you just imagined a break as well."

"It is nice to." Her eyes went to his sword. "Where did you get that sword?"

"It was made for me, a long time ago, by two very old friends."

"Are they still with us?"

His smile faltered and he fingered his sword. "No, sadly they are not. They died a long time ago."

"Oh, I'm sorry, it seems many people have lost loved ones. Wounds like that don't heal."

He shook his head sadly and "No they don't, many wounds don't heal."

"No they do not. Why do you think Luciana brought back her brother?"

"I don't—" he stopped and looked at her. There in her eyes was a familiar twinkle of mischievousness, something familiar in the way she said *her* name.

"I don't know."

"Hmm." She handed him the bucket of water. "Here have a drink."

"Thank you, I need one." He dumped the bucked on himself and Líead laughed making him smile. It was nice cold water.

She laughed. "Wow, if I had known you were going to pour it on yourself, I wouldn't have filled it up so much."

"I needed that actually. It's such a hot day, although the temperature is much cooler at night."

"It's the summer, what did you expect. It gets colder though, near the fortress."

"I know. It's because of the darkness, the death. Her presence always makes everything cold, stills the world around her."

"That may be, but it's easier to fight in the cold than it is in the heat. Maybe that's why she makes it cold. Who's knows." Líead pulled the bucked up from the well and dark some water.

"Maybe." He drank some and stared at her. "Líead, how long were you a slave to the elves?"

She shrugged. "I don't know, didn't really pay attention to time, just pretended that I was dead." She looked at him. "Why?"

"Curious."

"Hmm, well then, do you mind if I ask something?"

He smiled. "No, go ahead."

"It's nothing personal about you, but rather about one of your friends."

"Uh, okay."

"D–Galen, what did he lose? Or is it not your place to tell?"

"He wouldn't mind if I told you. He lost a daughter and a lover."

"Hmm, what a shame . . . what did you lose?"

"A mother a father a best friend, many in fact and a love. All of them lost to the darkness. What did you lose?"

"A family, a love."

"Everyone has lost something haven't they."

Her eyes turned cold. "Yes they have."

"Now what are the two of you doing out here late at night." Corbett and Líead jerked up. He knew that voice. He reached for his sword but stopped when an arrow hit the well next to his head. It was Damien.

"Ah, ah, ah, I don't think so thief." Nora came from the shadows before him shaking her finger at him disapprovingly. "Now what are you two doing?"

"We're sorry, we just wanted some water, it is a hot night, again we're sorry," said Líead bowing down, her hands on her knees.

He watched Nora look at Líead then stare at Corbett. Her blue eyes made his skin crawl. She smiled and tilted her head making her wavy blonde hair bounce in the process. She turned around and waved her hand.

"Go back to your rooms, before I change my mind." She walked away but he knew that Damien would shoot. Corbett grabbed Líead's hands and dragged her close to him.

"On the count of three, we need to start running," he whispered. She nodded an he began walking fast. He heard an arrow summoned.

"One–" The arrow was being pulled back. Wherever Damien was he was sure to have good aim.

"Two–" The arrow was loosened.

"Three–" They ran and the arrow barely missed them. As they ran Corbett heard Nora laugh as another arrow blew by their heads. Damien was toying with them.

Corbett pulled Líead along then finally dragged her into an alley way. He pressed his body against hers and they hid there in the darkness. He held her close and when he was sure they were gone he pulled away slightly and looked down at Líead.

Stop it Corbett, he told himself.

"Come on lets get going before they find us."

"Yeah okay."

He pulled her along after him and kept a look out as he lead the way back tp the Inn. Damn Nora to hell, damn them all, he thought. Maybe his curses helped he thought because they reached the inn alive.

"Are you okay?"

She nodded. "Yes, I'm fine." She turned around and headed for her room but stopped at the stairs. "Thank you for protecting me."

He smiled at her. "It was nothing, I would do anything for a friend." She smiled and began her walk up the stairs to her room.

Corbett sat down and rubbed his face and kept telling himself over and over again that pretty girls did not fall for cheap parlour tricks.

"Too many pretty girls, too many," and then finally he cracked and began laughing. Of all the things he was worried about, he was worried about too many pretty girls being a distraction.

Chapter Twenty-One

E ntia got out of bed and stroked her long black hair. Damn Nora, she almost had him confessing, but of course General "Princess" Nora had to have her fun, didn't she have enough to do trying to steal Damien away from Luciana. Entia sat up in bed and looked at her stuff already packed, probably by Cade. That's right they were leaving tonight. She had to tell Nora and Damian and of course Albin, he would have the most fun, but of course they were to let them all barely escape from battle, because of course, Luciana was to have her fun in the end.

She stretched and got out of bed. Entia took a bath and drowned herself in the water. She just wanted it all to be over, she wanted the battle to be done with and over, she wanted them dead already, just dead. Entia wanted her father dead by her sword.

She got some food and ate with Cade and Selene under the ever watchful eyes of Trixie who looked at her as though suspicious. Maybe I shouldn't have mentioned Silkas, she though, but then again, she should be able to have some fun too. She smiled at her and she smiled back. She looked around for Corbett and wondered if she could have anymore fun before they left for battle.

She gripped her fist. She could feel her immortality slipping free, could almost see the black strings of magic unbinding themselves. She tightened her grip, hoping to keep hold of the imaginary strands. Finally she looked at Selene, knowing Luciana, she would not be content with living as just reflection. She would take over and make it herself again. Then again, Selene already almost looked like her and there was that darkness inside her that even Luciana didn't know, that was alien even to her, but of course that intrigued her.

Selene looked at her and smiled. She smiled back then Corbett passed by and looked at her, but continued on his walk towards Coryn and Trixie. When Selene got up Entia took a sip of her drink and looked at Cade. She had to know.

"Cade, can I ask you something?"

"Of course."

"Do you ever get the feeling that Arlis and the rest are, I don't know, hiding something form us?"

He looked at her carefully and Entia saw it, in that one moment she saw and knew. Cade knew the truth.

"Well, sometimes I do, but I've known Tri—Nila for the longest that no matter what I think or feel, I will always trust her."

"Hmm, well if you trust them, so will I, besides Galen treats me like I am his daughter." She smiled and began to eat her breakfast. So she looked around and one specific person caught her eye and she wondered if he knew the truth.

*   *   *

Corbett watched Líéad through the corner of his eye. There was something about her, something familiar. There was also a strange beauty about her, an elfin beauty in the way she walked and talked and it felt familiar. Suddenly someone smacked him against the head.

"Stop staring at her Corbett," hissed Trixie.

He looked at her like he was twenty again, knowing no better. "Then who can I stare at . . . mom."

"Enough jokes. Corbett I don't trust her there something about her that's . . . cold."

"What did you expect, she watched people she trusted get slaughtered, people she loved."

"Corbett it's not like that. It's more like her heart is cold. It's the feeling of a general."

"But we would know if she were one disguised, we would sense the dark magic, it's our gift," he smiled and looked back at Líéad. "Besides, Nora and Damien almost killed her last night."

Trixie slapped his arm. "What do mean last night?! You were out with her? Alone?!"

"No, I woke up in a cold sweat, needed air and ran into her."

Trixie stared at him scrutinizing and rolled her eyes. "The closer we come to battle, the more childish you become. Why is that?"

He shrugged. "I don't know."

"It's your memories isn't it, your hope, the light inside you." A sad smiled appeared on her face as she looked at him. "It is beautiful I will admit, but alas, we need you as you were before . . . cold."

"I haven't changed, but I like having these moments when I can forget because once the battle comes and once it ends, I'll never be able to hide away in my memories."

She nodded understanding. "Do you think we'll win?"

"We have to, we don't really have a choice."

"Good point." She looked away from him and sighed sadly. "When are we going to tell them all who we really are, Selene especially?"

"I don't know, I haven't really given much thought to it, just though about running off and hiding as though—"

"As though you never existed? Yes I've thought about that as well, but what about our new friends, I don't think I could do it Corbett, and I don't think you would be able to either. Now pay our bill, for the day since we're leaving in the dead of night." She left him with that while he went to admiring every girl there, not to hide, but to forget who he was really thinking about.

*   *   *

Luciana felt miserable as she laid in bed, nothing could cure her. She had hid away in darkness for six centuries, collecting and stealing solders hee and there to unleash an army that could not be beat and *they* had never known.

Luciana had been sick for a while now and nothing could cure her. Not the darkness, not the despair, nor the death or the decay. So she lay in her dungeon room, the only place that could provide a type of cure for her. She needed to sever her tie with the light, with Corbett.

Her head ached, it had been aching for a while now. She looked down at her nails and could feel them tingle as they changed from black to jade to their natural colour. She clawed at her hair and the walls surrounding her. Something was fighting against her precious darkness inside her. Luciana heard someone down the hall and locked her cell door, blocking out all sounds with magic.

Luciana needed to go away, far away and wondered what her life would be like if she had run away when she was sixteen. Would she even be where she was now, hiding away in her dungeon? She looked around. He chained her here and tortured her, but the most painful was when he immobilized her and inserted the stone in her hand, letting her scream and bleed, and after she killed him, she escaped and ran back to her friends only to see them getting on with their lives. She punched the wall and watched the stone fall to the floor. She quickly fixed it back up, it had to be neat for the princess, of course her blood could stay, it was after all such a good touch.

Luciana traced her fingers over every crack on the dungeon. The chain immobilized the magic of magic users and she looked out through the bars. She saw the line clearly, the line separating the darkness from the light. It was so clear, so transparent. She teleported herself to the line, she stared ahead then remembered the dungeon. He carelessly snapped her fingers to end the spell that held the dungeon. She smiled in delight, she could already imagine their faces. She tapped her finger against the trees and turned them black.

"So you did poison my forest, how clever," said Isabelle standing by a tree.

"I was always better than you in magic, always ahead of you, except during that little time when you made them forget about me. I'll never let that happen again."

"Had I known you were this cold, I would have killed you myself and saved Corbett the tolerable agony of such an ending."

"You forget little sister dear," she hissed, "I wouldn't be so cold had you all come back and saved me! You left me to die! You let him torture me! You feel into his trap! Pawns, that's what you were and that's what you are again. My pawns this time." Luciana stroked her sisters' face then gripped her cheeks tightly. "What is worse than someone you love betraying you? How 'bout I tell you. Family, blood, that's what is far worse Bella. Think on that, your day of reckoning is coming."

"We'll destroy you."

Luciana laughed harshly. "And you still keep that hard shell wrapped so tightly, that mask unwavering about your face. I mist say it is amazing. Well goodbye little sister dear . . . for now." Luciana let her go and turned and walked away calmly. No arrow protruded her as she walked then looked back. "What, no arrow, I'm insulted." She laughed and continued on her way. Soon it would all come to an end.

*   *   *

Selene packed her bags and supplies, her head hurt. She sat down and looked at herself and hated what she saw. She saw Darkness, something she didn't like to see. She tapped her fingernails against the mirror and smiled, what ever it was that she had seen was probably due to Luciana and would fade when she did. She turned her back to it and looked back at her things.

"My you are pathetic," said a voice. Selene turned around slowly and in the mirror was Luciana. She tapped the glass. "I know you see me Selene. Please sit and talk for a while."

Selene willingly took a seat at the mirror and stared in strong. "What do you want?"

"Why don't you tell them that you talk to me, that we have these little conversations?"

"Because it's none of their concern."

"You are pathetic." She gripped the sides of Selene's mirror and slipped her hands out. Selene's direction shifted from each hand before returning back to Luciana's face.

"You could kill me in my sleep, me and Edel, why haven't you?"

"Now where would the fun be in that? Let me tell you something, this may be a battle to you, but it's nothing more than a game to me." She tilted her head. "I see your packing. Leaving so soon, I must say that is a disappointment, really. Well in any case," she snatched Selene's face and pulled it close to the mirror, "I should leave before Corbett comes to your rescue, as always, give him a message for my Corbett. Tell him that I've got you . . . actually better yet, tell him that I will defeat him."

"Is that all?"

"My, my, aren't you an obedient one."

"If it will get your disgusting hands off my face, then yes of course I am to your every demand." she said hatefully,

"Such impotence, really, you are a treasure."

"Get off me you witch!"

"Lower your voice, I would hate to accidentally snap your neck, I mean that would be such a shame considering you are their last hope."

"Let me go."

"Say please and we'll see what happens."

"*Please* let me go."

Luciana let go and Selene quickly took a step back, knocking over her chair in the process. Why did Luciana think she knew Corbett, who was he.

"What is it princess."

"I pity you."

Luciana stared at her coldly. "Why?"

"Because, what ever happened to turn you into this must have been very heartbreaking."

A chill went down her spine when Luciana smiled coldly. "You think you understand don't you."

"You must have been weak–" She stopped and flinched when Luciana punched the mirror.

"You know nothing!" She vanished and Selene smiled. She achieved in making her leave.

Selene bent down and picked up the glass from the mirror and fixed it with magic. She wouldn't tell anyway what Luciana had said, no one needed to know, she was their last hope, she needed them to believe that she was fine or else what else was there left to believe in.

Selene sat on her bed and waited for Edel to come up. She had to talk to him, she said she needed to talk to him. A knock came and she knew who it was. He smiled and took her breath away.

"Selene?"

"Edel, come here I need to speak to you." He made an indescribable face but walked over to her nonetheless.

"Edel I love you, and I can tell that you love me so please just tell me, because I need to know for sure."

"Selene I . . . I do love you but—"

"Shh, that's all I need to know." Selene kissed him. She knew that she was not going to get another chance to do so. She sat on him and kissed him some more. Edels hands wrapped around her waist and she loved it. All she wanted was him nothing more. Selene slipped off his shirt and looked into his eyes.

"Edel—"

"Selene—" He pushed her off him and ruffled his hair. "Selene, I can't, I just can't. I'm sorry, it's just I can't, not with so much going on. I'm sorry I just can't Selene."

"Edel—"

He grabbed his shirt and walked out and Selene stared at the doorway. She didn't know what just happened. Edel said he loved her then left her. She got up and shoved her last pair of pants into her back.

"Edel . . . what's going on."

Later on, in the dead of night, Selene barely made her contact with Edel as they began to sneak off into the night.

As they approached the end of the town, standing at the end of the bend stood Albin, Nora and Damien. Selene stared transfixed at her little brother.

"Hello Princess," said Nora, "how fare thee?"

"You royal bitch! Give me back my brother!" Selene got off her horse before Líead could stop her. Selene only got as far as three steps towards them when an arrow entered her side.

"Selene!"

"Don't you ever call me that. I am not your brother you evil witch!" Albin lowered his quiver. Nora and Damien exchanged glanced and stared at Albin.

"Albin stand down," said Damien.

"I should kill her."

"Those we're not your mothers orders!" said Nora.

"Albin, she's not your mother! *Our* mother was—"

"Shut up!" Albin pulled out his sword and ran to her. He grabbed her hair and pulled her back, away from her friends. The arrow broke off but the head of it flew deeper inside her. Albin pulled her to her knees and put his sword on her neck.

"Albin please!"

"Albin let her go," said Nora.

"I should kill you!"

"Please no!"

"Let her go," said Edel, his sword drawn.

"Give me a good reason why I shouldn't kill her?"

He jerked her head back. Selene screamed, she could feel the arrow head inch further inside her.

"Because I say so son." Luciana stepped from the shadows and walked over to Albin smiling. She bent down and whispered something in his ear. He shoved Selene to the ground and sheathed his word. Nila ran to her and Líead followed her, sword drawn.

"Either kill us or let us pass," said Arlis.

"Oh, I have no intention of you killing you just yet. Have a safe journey," she looked down at Selene. "You should probably help her, most of my arrows are tipped with poison." She laughed and vanished along with Nora, Damien and Albin.

Chapter Twenty-Two

S elene screamed. Corbett made a fire and watched her. Trixie looked up at him and left her with Líead and over to him.

"Well?"

"The arrow head has gone in deeper. We need magic to save her, to pull it out, then I'm going to have to boil an antidote and pour it on her, while it's fresh, but I need the arrow for the antidote, I need to know the poison."

"Crap, what are you trying to say Trixie?"

"She may not live long enough."

"No, she has to, Luciana, this—"

"Breath Corbett, breath."

"Donovan you know magic, gather others that do and save her dammit, I don't want any excuses." He wiped his hands over his face and turned his back to everyone. He needed the antidote now, *she* needed the antidote now.

Corbett walked off and punched a nearby tree. He suddenly just began pulling at all the flowers and weeds from the ground and shove them into his bag. He continued his madness until his bag was full and stood for a moment longer.

"Give me the antidote," he begged.

"No," came her voice. He clenched his fist.

Corbett ran back to the fire and ignored the gazes cast on him, and shoved his pack into Trixie's arm.

"Do what you can, I don't want any excuses. Save her life—NOW!" Trixie flinched but didn't make any movement to do what he had just ordered making Corbett's anger grow, makign him tempted to slap her. He took a step closer to her. "Nila . . . GET MOVING!" She flinched again, tok a step back but did not move.

"Nila, so help me I don't slap you. Now I'm going to say this one more time. Get moving, save her life. Understand?"

"I can't. The arrow__"

"Get it out!" He walked over to Donovan and dragged him over. "Get it out."

"It's–"

"Get it out . . . NOW!"

* * *

Luciana watched in amusement as did Albin. The poison was not deadly, it would fade when the arrow did, it would do the girl no harm. She enjoyed how Corbett fussed and got violent with his old friends. He would blow his cover if he kept it up. Poor pitiful Corbett, she thought happily. Her arrow would vanish once it touched darkness, the darkness that both frightened and mesmerized her. She needed his untouched power, she ached for it.

Luciana tapped her hand against the glass and leaned forward to look at her. Selene screamed in pain and agony. Donovan sat over her trying to use magic but it would not work and he knew that. There was nothing they could do but allow her to suffer through the pain, the agony.

"Mom, how much longer will this be, not that I don't enjoy this," he smiled.

"I'm not sure, but I hope soon. I need the know, what has unleashed this darkness."

"Are you sure it wasn't you?"

She nodded. "It's unfamiliar, I can't place it, but I know of it, it intrigues me darling."

"Hmm, it is intriguing."

She looked at him briefly. "I haven't complimented you on your performance yet. It was brilliant."

He bowed. "Thank you moth-majesty, but can I ask, why didn't you inform Nora or Damien?"

She laughed. " I simply wanted to see the reaction on their faces, besides they would have given the operation away." Albin nodded and sat down.

"Albin, I hope you know, it is her body I will be taking."

"I know, but it will be you and you will use your magic to shape her into you."

"True, I will." She hugged him dearly and went back to the show in her mirror.

*   *   *

Trixie couldn't do anything, the poison had already spread through out her body, I was only a matter of time till it reached her heart and stopped it. She looked down at Donovan who was muttering spell after spell to try and save her. Six hundred years worth and still not a spell worked.

She remembered Corbett, how the madness showed in his eyes. It looked as though the darkness can completely taken over, but she knew better, he was just frightened. Trixie knelt down and rubbed some of the oils onto her wound, for the time being. She grabbed her bowl and canteen and mixed up some more flowers till they were one compound, before smearing some onto her wound. Selene screamed. Donovan looked at her but she continued anyway, the least she could do was sooth the pain.

"Trixie, she's dying, there's nothing we can do!"

"I know, but Corbett isn't in his right mind at the moment, and I don't blame him. She's our only hope—"

"Was," corrected Donovan.

"She's not dead yet Donovan. And you wonder why Adira and Entia hate you."

"Trixie—"

"No, *we* have to be strong, have hope even where none lies."

He stared at her and nodded, then returned to the spell casting. Trixie went back to smearing and praying that all would be well.

*   *   *

Selene didn't know what all the fuss was about. She wasn't in pain, it didn't hurt. So why was she screaming. She heard the names Donovan and Corbett and Trixie, but she couldn't see who was talking, all voices were distant. She screamed again for no reason. She couldn't feel any pain Everything was so cloudy, so blurred, incoherent.

At long last something touched her. Whatever it was felt powerful, felt good. It was dark, darker than Luciana, but it felt distant, untapped. Selene shivered and stared at it. No, she would not let this darkness consume her, she would not become Luciana.

*   *   *

Luciana found it. She smiled and sat back in the chair. What will power this young girl had, such a will to walk away from the power, away from the tempting darkness that could consume her.

"Mother?"

"I found her darkness, it's both alien yet familiar."

"Is that good or bad?"

"Neither Albin, it just is."

"What do you mean?"

"Nothing for the time being. Hmm, Albin go get Nora."

"Okay." He stood up, his armour silent as he walked from the room. She stared at the mirror and snapped her fingers. She would end the spell, after another few hours.

"You called Luciana," asked Nora.

Luciana looked ta her and smiled. "I found the darkness."

"So now what."

"Now we'll let her come to us of course."

"Hmm."

"Oh you still aren't upset are you?"

"You didn't inform us . . . me in particular."

"It was far more convincing that way. I found it rather amusing."

"I'm glad you did. Damien seemed to think so as well."

"Stop being so sour and get rid of twenty men, I don't care of what calvary just do it."

"Why?"

"Even out the battle." She smiled and Nora did as well.

"As you wish majesty." Nora bowed turning sharply on her heels and walked out.

*   *   *

Corbett walked around blindly. He had no idea where he was only that he was away. Selene couldn't die she just couldn't, he told himself. Oh Luciana, don't make me kill you, please, I want to save you not kill you. He laid down and stared up at the sky. He couldn't fall asleep not with the threat of Luciana or his Luci showing up and clouding his mind, although she did that anyway and enjoyed it heavily.

Corbett sighed, he had to admit every time he saw her, he loved it. It reminded him of the past of how good everything used to be, of how wonderful it used to be. How he used to just ride out of nowhere and sweep her off her feet, away from the other village boys. Maybe he always had loved her, he was stupid to even try to think otherwise. She had always acted upset, but he had always known better, she thought all the village boys were pigs, if nothing less, and enjoyed the rescue.

"Can I save you?"

"You can try." Corbett turned and stared at Coryn.

"Why aren't you with Selene and the others?"

"Because you were acting ridiculous. Corbett nothing they are doing is helping. All we have is hope."

Corbett looked away hatefully, the word stinging in his ears. "Hope does nothing, it is just a word."

Coryn shook his head sadly. "You're wrong Corbett, hope is everything. Without hope why are we fighting, risking not only our lives but the lives of others?"

"Because it is the right thing Coryn, just because it is the right thing."

Coryn waved his arms in frustration. "Have you lost sight to everything! You must have if you really believe that it the only reason."

Corbett shot him a hateful glare. "Go away Coryn . . . now!"

"Fine, but just think about it Corbett, or else what's the point of fighting."

"Go away." Corbett turned away and closed his eyes. No, hope was nothing, just a thought, a word used when all is lost. Hope was nothing.

*　　*　　*

Entia watched everything. She knew this was all fake, the poison would vanish soon enough, one the Darkness Luciana was so fond of and of course when she was done having her fun.

Her father kept muttering his stupid spells and Trixie kept smearing on the ointment. She looked down at Selene. She was pale as nice, a nice little touch, as well as the screaming. Oh Luciana you are brilliant. She hid her smile beneath her feigned face of distress and continued to watched on. Of course her father looked up and stared at her, watched her. Her faze didn't waver, she would not waver, she would kill him in cold blood like he killed Silkas. She willingly went to Luciana for the chance to kill her father and her one true love followed her and fought by her side, and Donovan had taken the chance at his mortality and murdered him. She had watched him die and tried to save him, tried to run to him but it was to late. He died before she reached him, before anyone had had the chance of reaching him.

Cade reached for her hand and held it tightly and Entia looked at him and wondered if history would repeat itself. She smiled at Cade, hopeful. No probably not, Silkas had been truly in love with her, would die for her and did. His death turned Adira against Donovan which Entia took total advantage of. Adira was her creation, as well as Donovan's creation. Cade wouldn't be blinded by love, he had more sense than that, more good in him, not a touch of darkness that could consume him.

"Líead, are you all right? I mean I know how much you and Selene have gotten to know each other but I'm worried about you are you okay? I mean she might die," said Cade all to concerened.

Entia stared at him and smiled. "She won't die."

"You don't—"

"It's not about knowing anything Cade, it's about having hope and faith."

He stared at her and kissed her suddenly. She was a brilliant actress, and besides she should have some fun. She was entitled to it after all.

*   *   *

Donovan didn't like what he felt, the strong force behind it, something was not right. He looked up and saw Líead staring and he stared back. Her stare was blank, her face was blank. After all she had been through, of course she could easily hide her emotions. But there was something wrong with her story. Silkas was a branded name as was Entia. Entia who had gone over willingly, with no questions asked, and her Silkas who had died following her. There were too many similarities between her and his daighter. Those names were branded taboo, nothing and no one was to say them or be named with them.

Cade arrived and distracted her. Líead really liked him, and he saw it, they all saw it, and Cade liked her back. Donovan couldn't help but feel protective of her, the daughter he could have had, could have raised. He killed his daughter, turned both his daughter and Adira, his love, against him. Silkas death and sealed his fate, to watch the two he loved the most turn into monsters.

"I'm sorry Entia," he mumbled under his breath.

Chapter Twenty-Three

Only she could see him for what he really was. He was a mad man, he was finally her equal. Luciana tapped her finger against the glass and watched as she rode away alongside his companions. Donovan of course had to use his magic to modify memories of the madness. Luciana continued to tap her finger.

Her fist convulsed and her nails dug into the glass as she dragged them across the mirror, making that blood letting sound. She hated him with a passion. He betrayed her, they all did. In her anger Luciana smashed her mirror with her fist and sat there against her window and looked over her vast kingdom. It was all hers. The Elfin Kingdom, the whole Kingdom was hers. Then the thought of betrayal crossed her mind as her eyes passed over her sisters tavern. The betrayal of blood. The air around her chilled and she waved her hand and repaired the mirror newly covered with a thin layer of frost. Lets see what my little sister is up to, she thought. A knock came distracted her from her fun and she waved it open.

"Luci, how fare thee?" said Damien mockingly.

"Hello Damien." He closed the door and walked over to her.

"So how are you?"

"Fine, contemplating the theory of the betrayal of the blood. It's quite exuberating," she said sarcastically.

Damien looked down at her and smiled. "You are so cynical."

"So I've been told."

"Hmm . . . she's jealous of you," said Damien rather suddenly.

"Now why would Nora be jealous of me?"

"What makes you think I'm talking about her?" She gave him a look accompanied with a smile and he laughed. "It's because I love, because everyone loves you."

Luciana laughed harshly and sat down on her bed. "Not everyone Damien." Suddenly Damien kissed her and held her tightly. Luciana knew what he was doing, he was trying to make her forget, which she loved all too much. She loved him, she loved Nathaniel but her love for Corbett was true and undeniable. He was Corbett after all, her best friend. Luciana would have succumbed to the temptation had she not remembered Corbett.

"Not today Damien."

"Still contemplating the concept of betrayal."

She shared his smiled and looked down. "As always yes." She kissed him once again. "Go kill some men Damien and please make sure that they are *men* and not elves, I prefer the elves for battle."

"As you wish." He stood up and bowed before leaving the room.

Luciana layed down on her bed and took from her night stand her black orb that had had once belonged to Nora. It was all happening again so very beautifully, it will happen again and this time she would be victorious – indefinitely.

*   *   *

Once upon a time – Selene sighed as they rode along clutching her stomach remembering the stories her mother sued to tell her. If only her life was like those fairy tales – there lived a princess who's family was slaughtered before her eyes as she was forced to hide away and run away with the boy she loved – Edel. She sighed again. No her life wasn't much of a fairy tale – and for a time—seven years—they travelled around forming an army to try to defeat the queen, the Dark Empress—Luciana—and when the battle finally came—But Selene didn't know if her story would have a happy ending. She didn't know how it would end. She didn't even know how the day would end.

It had been several days since her brother had shot her with an arrow, temporarily incapacitating her. Everyone thoughts where a bit muffled and, maybe that was because of how everyone remembered things, or rather didn't remember.

Selene looked at Edel and he smiled at her warmly. Not even he remembered little bits and pieces. That told her that something was amiss, that Donovan, Coryn, Trixie and especially Corbett had something to do with it. Those people who continued to ruin her life.

Of course she sighed again. She missed Isabelle who like herself and Líead had suffered a loss at the hands of Luciana. She couldn't wait to see her again, she missed her so much, and they were only three weeks away.

Líead shifted in her saddle and Selene looked at her. She looked anxious and tired, like she was waiting for something. They all were but she looked the most anxious, and pale, as though she were sick. She looked as though she was poisoned. Selene gripped her tighter and Líead looked at her confused, then smiled and Selene saw something she had never seen before, a sort of true happiness that made her purple eyes light up.

"Líead," said Nila riding up next to them.

"Yes?"

"Do you have any elf in you?"

Selene felt Líead shift and stiffen. "One-eight, yes, how did you know?"

"You're sight and keen hearing. It's not common for humans, I don't care even if you did grow up among elves."

"Why does my heritage matter Nila?"

"I agree with Líead, why does it matter?"

"Because purple eyes are not common."

"What are you saying? What do my eyes have to do with anything?" Entia was growing frightened. Luciana would kill her if she messed up.

"You may be a descendant of General Entia," and with that she rode forward.

"Líead don't–"

"Don't worry, about it Selene, it really is no big deal, whether I am a descendant or not isn't really my concern, I am who I am and that cannot be changed." She smiled and Selene did as well. Líead would never betray them, that much Selene could tell.

*   *   *

Entia bitterly had to admit that she liked Selene and Cade, but then again, she wouldn't mind seeing them die. She smiled to herself then caught Trixie staring at her. She knew nothing about who she was, had only suspicions. Of course maybe Entia shouldn't have brought up Silkas' name. Again she smiled, that temptation had been to sweet to be passed.

"Líead," said Selene.

"Yes?"

"Can you tell me about Silkas? About your life before?"

Líéad stared at her shocked. "Uh, sure, of course. Well the town I was born into was small town, like any other small town. My mother, she had chestnut hair and brilliant blue eyes, like the ocean. My father was mayor, a pleasantry. Silkas lived with us. His name was considered taboo, so even though he was loved by many, he and his family were exiled for breaking the law."

Selene gave her a confused look. Of course they wouldn't have told her about the generals and their past. "Why is the name taboo?"

"Because Silkas was the name of General Entia's love, her fiancé who turned to darkness willingly to follow his love. But his parents couldn't resist because the name means beloved and they had always had trouble conceiving, so they broke the law and cherished him."

"Oh."

"Yes, sad in a way, bitter sweet I guess. Now they loved him, everyone loved him and cherished him, my family even more so, taking them in when they had no place else to go. Silkas had even helped with my birth." She laughed. "He would always admire my growth. I always laughed because he never aged a day. That always made him laugh."

"How old was he when you two got engaged?"

"He was two-hundred and thirty-six. That was a funny story."

"Why?"

"Because he wouldn't ask me to marry him. He didn't want to watch me waste away while he didn't. I said that I didn't care and kissed him. He pushed me away then kissed me. We were to be wed in the spring."

Selene smiled at her. "That's sweet."

"Isn't it. My two little brothers all while I was growing up were the most annoying troublesome children that I would never trade for anything." Entia made a shadow of sadness cloud her face. She was having fun. Then she thought if she should mention it. No, then Trixie would be completely adamant on her thoughts of who she was and would expose her. She looked up at Trixie and Donovan who where watching her intently. She just rode on her horse and gripped her reins.

"Hey Arlis!"

"Yeah."

"Do you mind if we ride on ahead? We'll set up camp."

"Well I—"

"Please Arlis."

"Yes, please Arlis," said Selene.

"Okay, sure why not. Cade go with them."

"All right." He smiled and Entia and Selene smiled back.

"We'll race you Cade." And with that Entia galloped away followed by Cade and they all were filled with laughter. Oh well so death will come to them at least it will be fun.

*   *   *

Trixie rode up to Corbett along with Donovan. Corbett looked at Coryn who looked aside then rolled his eyes and stared at Trixie.

"What now?"

"Do you remember what happened, why it took us so long to go and lose Luci to him."

His anger fuelled him and he gripped her wrist. "Don't you dare call her Luci, not now not ever."

"Let go of me." She snatched her wrist away then stared at him. "Now, never mind that, right now do you remember why we had to stop?"

"Yes. Entia was with child and Donovan would not let us, and neither would Silkas nor you or Adira or even Esmerelda, continue on with our journey until she gave birth. So we waited for seven months which aggravated her."

"Do you remember what happened with the child?"

"You ran her back to the kingdom where she was then queen after you faked her death." Corbett trotted along and rolled his eyes. He didn't see the point of remembering the past. And Trixie was constantly bothering on about it.

"Corbett, do you remember that she sent her daughter into hiding?"

"Get to your damn point Trixie."

"I think Líead is her descendant, I just believe in it so much."

"Doesn't make sense, especially since we know where her granddaughter is." He looked at her. "What do you want me to do, ask her if she has had any indiscretions?"

"Yes, but I don't think I have a choice on the matter."

"No you don't. Besides, why does it matter if she is or not?"

"It just does all right," she said hotly.

"Trixie I need you to relax and calm down. You're not thinking clearly."

Trixie stared at him angrily. "You're one to talk." Quickly Coryn and Donovan rode between them.

"Enough you two," said Donovan.

"Yeah, you two have been fighting far too much," continued Coryn. "We're not enemies here, we're friends."

"We know," they said in unison, Corbett looked at Trixie unwaveringly in the eyes who stared back at him in anger. Finally he rode forward, away from her and her stupid paranoia.

Chapter Twenty-Four

Cade and Selene were sound asleep so of course she took a little walk and called for Luciana who slipped out of a shadow. Fatigue covered her face but a smile was there nonetheless.

"You like her don't you? And him."

"I find them tolerable."

"I don't blame you, I myself find her admirable."

"Do you now, hmm, as do I, but why do you? What is is about her that admires you so? Why her body and I know it's more than the magic. There are many more mages, more powerful then her, more fair, so why her?"

"Because she reminds me of me. Before all of this of course."

"Any regrets?"

All of her fatigue vanished and she looked at her, all the while poisoning a tree. "None."

"Of course."

"There is a little point that if I take over her it will destroy them all, him especially."

"True."

Luciana stared at her impassively. She knew that there was more to this. "Why did you call me? I know it wasn't to chat about regrets and our . . . admiration."

"Yes well—" Entia fidgeted and Luciana walked over to her as she stared down at her feet, frightened. "I may have messed up." Luciana sudden cold grip on her neck stung her and she could feel herself being raised into the air.

"Define messed up Entia."

Entia struggled in her grasp and kicked about.

"I mentioned Silkas. It is—is only Trixie who suspects anything," she managed to cough up. "She thinks that I may be my great-granddaughter or something. Please Luciana 'messed up' was the wrong use of words."

Luciana dropped her and Entia fell to the ground gasping for air. She had forgotten just how cold and brutal she could be.

Luciana looked down at her and knelt down yanking Entias' head back by her hair.

"Don't screw up Entia, I mean it. They need to reach Isabelle without suspicion, talk to Trixie, fix this, now." She let her go and vanished. Entia clutched her throat remembering that she was like Nathaniel, Adira and Luciana, broken at heart before turned. That meant that Luciana could kill her, or worse, make her mortal.

*   *   *

Corbett trotted along waiting for a sign of Líead who said she would set up camp. He was glad she went on ahead, it gave them all incentive to travel farther on.

"Hey! Over here!"

Corbett turned his head and in the trees waving at them were Líead and Selene. He smiled and trotted along over to the, followed by everyone else.

"Nice spot."

"Isn't it, I chose it all by my little old self." Líead laughed as did Selene and Cade. Corbett smiled at their laughter and smiles, thinking how beautiful they were. It was something he would always remember.

"So how far is this place from Isabelle," asked Selene.

"Still far. But closer. Took us a day and a half to reach you—"

"Yes, thank you Líead," mocked Trixie bitterly.

"That's enough Nila," yelled Selene. Corbett looked at her then at Líead who stared at her.

"Selene—" began Líead.

"No," she said shaking her off, "I've had enough. This is not fair the way you are treating her! Líead is our comrade, our friend, and the way you are treating her is unacceptable and cruel and rude and I will not have it!"

"Selene that's enough," said Líead finally taking her shoulders and turning her towards her. "Enough. Everyone, camp is this way." She looked at Corbett and walked away with Selene to the camp sight. Everyone followed except the four.

"You know she's right," said Donovan. Corbett nodded in agreement containing his anger for Trixie. They did not need to start another argument now. "I agree as well," said Coryn. "We're all friends here, you should be nice." "I don't trust her."

"Why, just because her eyes are purple and she fell in love with an elf named Silkas. Coincidences happen Trixie, now enough of this madness," said Donovan. Corbett stared at Donovan. He really did care about the girl and Trixie herself was digging up horrible memories and emotions.

"Donovan—"

"You are going to talk her and apologize, understood."

"Of course, I'm sorry." They walked away and Corbett just watched Trixie as she stood embarrassed.

*   *   *

Luciana slipped into her tower and sat down before her ingredients. "Daniel!" she screamed. He appeared and stared at her.

"Yes?"

"I need you to undo Donovan' magic. Entia is doing very well creating discord, but it's not good enough. Donovan is blocking the memory of Corbett's madness."

"Well that's not fair." He laughed and sat down taking up a vial. "I'm sure I can concoct something." He looked at her and his amber eyes stared at her deeply. He was the only one who made her feel uneasy. He knew every aspect of the curse, inside and out.

"Daniel," she said getting up to avoid his gaze. "I need you to train Albin in every aspect of this curse . . . spell."

"Why?"

"He needs to know that we aren't invulnerable, that we have but one pathetic weakness. He needs to know so he won't get himself killed."

"Very productive."

"I know." She was about to send him out of the room when something crossed her mind. "Daniel, go bless my armour, one can never be to careful."

"Especially in these dire times."

Lucian snapped around furious. "These are not dire times!"

"Ah but they are. Our immortality is running thin and a sort of realization is beginning to dawn on Corbett. Be mindful though, that thought, although it has yet to fully manifest itself the threat does exist there."

She growled and her talons enlarged. "He will not discover anything – ever."

"Maybe not, but be warned, that treat does live within him."

"Go work on Albin and that potion, immediately." He simply bowed then left the room. She tapped her mirror and he came forth.

"Yes?"

"Is he right? Is Daniel right?!"

He looked on her calmly. "You already know the answer to that my dear, if you didn't you wouldn't be here asking now would you." Luciana wanted to strangle him and couldn't contain herself, she punched the glass meaning to strangle him but nothing happened, a simple crack formed and her hand began to bleed, she could feel the blood drip down her fingers. Her wounds were taking longer and longer to heal.

His lordship simply snapped his fingers and the crack vanished. She stared at him coldly.

"I was your secret to immortality," said finally after a few minutes of desired silence.

"True immortality cannot be achieved in a body."

Her anger emanated outside of her body, filling the room with power. "What happens to me then?! I don't want to rule from behind glass. I want to rule!"

"You will see you take over her body when . . . if Corbett kills you. There is a darkness there that once you inhabit, you can consume and become her, take over her, shape the body to be you, what you are now."

"That darkness? That same darkness that frightens even you?! And what happens to me! What if it consumes even me?!"

"You will not be consumed. I know you won't. That day you touched it, something in it stirred as though it was alive itself. Darkness likes darkness, feeds off darkness, grows off darkness. When s shadow touches another shadow, it grows. You power will grow."

Luciana clutched her fists and stared at the mirror angrily, uncertain. "You had better be sure because it if I become stuck behind that glass with you, I promise you, you will regret it for all eternity."

"I'm sure I will." He vanished without another word. Only power could save her now. Only darkness could maker her triumphant against her pathetic betrayers.

❉   ❉   ❉

Trixie looked for Líead. Donovan was right in the end. They couldn't afford to be divided, not it they wanted to win anyway, not if they wanted to defeat their once close friend and loved ones.

It wasn't right, she wasn't right. Donovan was right and so because of that she looked for Líead. After searching here and there she finally found her, sitting up in a tree like an elf.

"Líead?"

Líead didn't look down but instead kept her gaze towards the sky and simply said, "what have I done now?" Líead looked down before Trixie could say anything and had a simply elegant smile on her face. "I must have done something wrong it you came all the way out here to find me."

Trixie didn't particularly care for her tone but knew she deserved it nonetheless.

"No, you haven't done anything wrong not in the least. I am the one who has, and I have come looking for you to apologize to you about something. Actually I came to apologize for the way I have been treating you."

She watched Líead's eyes open in shock. "Really, you came to apologize?"

"Yes. I have been treating you very poorly and with no justifiable cause either. You've done nothing wrong, on the contrary, you've been more than great, especially where Selene is concerned."

Líead looked her up and down, analysing her. "Hmm, you're only apologizing because Donovan told you to didn't he."

"No——" Trixie stopped and stared at her frightened. "What did you just say."

"No need to play coy Trixie, you know very well what I said."

"How do you—"

"I listen. You think everyone is asleep when their not. You four have become very careless and cocky."

"Have you—"

"No, I haven't told Selene, but what I'm trying to understand is why you haven't." She jumped down from the tree and stared at her directly in her eyes.

"She hates us. She blames us for the death of her family, for the turn of her brother."

"She wouldn't if you would just explain to her the consequences of what happened. She would hate you at first, that is true, but in the end, she would understand that you had nothing to do with the destruction of Radiance, with the death of her family."

"How are you so sure?"

"Because I know Selene. She is kind and strong and listens to what people have to say. You don't give her enough credit." She walked off and Trixie stood her ground, staring straight ahead. Maybe Líead was right.

"You are forgiven by the way," she heard Líead say behind her.

Alone she knew she was as she listened to the dew fall off the leaves. She could not decide if Líead was a threat or just a helpful friend. Líead frightened her. She had suspected something, but in the end she had been honest with her. But her gaze, her purple eyes, the intensity reminded her of Entia, everything about her reminded her about Entia. Finally she decided that at the moment she would trust her and inform the others.

Chapter Twenty-Five

S elene was relieved to see the tavern, Isabelle's tavern. It was a nice thought, that she would get to sleep in a warm bed again. She smiled blissfully and looked at Edel who smiled back at her. Soon it would all be at an end. Soon, she would get to live peacefully with Edel.

She tied up her horse and looked inside through one of the windows. There was large crowd in there, approximately thirty people by the looks of it. Her smiled grew even more grand. She saw Isabelle serving pints to the people here and there and then address others for food. Her eyes grew even wider when she noticed a young man with an apparent keen interest in Isabelle.

"She looks happy," said Edel who was suddenly next to her.

Selene was slightly startled by his sudden appearance but nodded and smiled. "She does. I can't wait to say hi to her again. I've missed her.'

"Well it has been seven years Selene. Come on, lets go say hi."

Selene was so overjoyed. She ran to the front door and ran in. She knew that everyone was probably staring at her like she was mad. But recognition covered Isabelle's face.

"My, my Selene, it is a pleasure to see you. Took you guys long enough to get here."

"We ran into a lot of trouble on the way," said Arlis setting his stuff down.

"Well we've been having trouble here too. Have you noticed the trees? They are all turning black. She's poisoned the whole area, and she didn't do it alone." She looked around. "Is this all?" she said rather disappointed.

"People are scared Isabelle," stated Selene. "They fear for their lives as well as that of loved ones, you can't blame them."

A hard look covered Isabelle. "They should put aside their selfishness for the greater good. It's not fair that people that we—"

"Enough Isabelle," said Arlis. "We all need to relax for a few nights. We've been travelling almost non-stop for almost two months."

"Of course. I've got many beds made and as you can tell *I've* expanded," she said smuggly looking at Arlis. Finally she turned back to Selene and a gently smile covered her usually hard face. "Go get some rest."

Selene smiled and ran up the stairs. She soon found herself immersed in blankets and dreams.

It was not, however, a pleasant night as she had hoped. It was of that time when she had been unconscious, shot with a poison arrow by her dead brother. Voices were heard, those of Nila, Arlis and Galen. Something was happening and someone was angry.

Selene jolted awake and looked around. Edel lay peacefully, sound asleep next to her. Selene lay back down and watched him as his chest rose up and down in rhythmic motions. It was a nice thing to see; a loved one alive.

*　　*　　*

Luciana watched them as Entia administered the potion to all as she helped Isabelle serve the food and drinks. It was a pleasant thing to see, all those she despised reliving their grave mistake.

Luciana especially took great care to study the elf girl taken in by Isabelle. Her eyes were a bright purple and her features were almost fine like Entia. It's her granddaughter of course she realized. She should only be a few centuries old, probably three hundred at least.

"Daniel?"

"Yes," he said as he materialized.

"Isn't that your daughter?"

He looked at the mirror and smiled. "I believe it is."

"Good," she looked at him, "where's her mother?"

He shrugged carelessly. "I don't know. Dead I presume. It would seem to be the most logical conclusion."

Luciana looked at the glass and at Entia. "Pity. Does Entia know that that is your daughter?"

"I don't even think she even realizes her existence there. She's not as observant as you."

Luciana looked at him as he walked out of the room and remembered the day she met him. He had not liked any of them at their first encounter, not in the least.

Luciana, Damien and Corbett had taken a look ahead. Entia was going to give birth soon, but there was nothing any of them could do.

"I remember this place," said Damien. "I think I should stay here."

Luciana pinched him playfully. "Whatever you did, they have to forget. Entia is going to give birth soon. Her pregnancy has already delayed us too much. This is where she will give birth, in this town, in a bed."

"But—"

"Enough," said Corbett. "Do you know anyone?"

He nodded. "Someone, yes, but he's not particularly fond of me, pure blood bastard."

"An elf?" questioned Corbett.

"Not just any elf, Daniel, he's a wizard in training . . . almost, very perceptive though. I hate him."

Luciana laughed. "And why is that? Because he's a pureblood or because he's a wizard?"

"Both, but the feeling is mutual."

"Why?" asked Corbett.

"You don't need to know."

"Ah but we do," began Luciana. "We need to know so that, if it's even possible, we can stand up for you, or manipulate him, which ever I'm in the mood for," she laughed and Corbett smiled.

"He doesn't like me because I grew up here and I'm a half-blood who couldn't and more importantly wouldn't love his arrogant twin sister. She was beautiful yes, but intolerable,, simply obnoxious, with no discretion what so ever. To put it bluntly she was—"

"A slut?' finished Luciana smiling.

"Yes."

"Well now, I'll pretend to be your wife and Corbett my brother." She smiled and him and he frowned.

They followed Damien as he led the way to the house. He hesitated lengthily at the door. Luciana in her impatience knocked and grabbed Damien's arm. A young elf man appeared and stood glaring at Damien.

"You! What are you doing here?" Daniel growled. Luciana though quickly stepped in between them, protecting Damien.

"Hello I'm Luciana. We are travelling with a friend who is about to give birth and she needs a bed—"

"I don't care, anyone who has to do with *him* can rot."

Corbett saw Luciana eyes tweak in annoyance and pulled Damien a step back. Damien stared at Corbett confused, but Corbett had seen that look before, that annoyance, and the after effect was never pleasant.

"Ugh, I don't have time for this." She waved her hand and knocked Daniel to his feet and walking in, a green in her eyes shining brightly. "Please let us in."

"Get out." He shot a spell at her but she simply blocked it.

"I guess I have failed to mention that we are travelling with the Princesses Esmerelda and Trixie."

He spat at her feet. "We don't live in the elven kingdom, so I care not of their presence, or their rule," retorted Daniel.

"Hmm, well then I guess I should have mentioned that I'm travelling with Princess Nora and Prince Coryn."

"Brother!" cried a female voice. The girl looked so much like her brother that she presumed that this must have been his twin. Luciana waved her into a seat as she passed one, running to aid her brother, and held her down.

"Please, sit."

"What the—"

"Damien go get the others, we seem to have found the most perfect house."

"Okay." He ran and Corbett closed the door behind him.

"So what now?" he asked.

"I'm not sure, I'm just living in the moment." She laughed and Corbett smiled.

"You're them aren't you?" asked Daniels' sister. "The small pathetic rebellion?"

Luciana turned towards her and shared an alarming look with Corbett who was quickly pulling out his sword.

"Who are you?" he demanded.

"One of his minions." She smiled. "You can't defeat him, in the end you'll just become one of his pons, a puppet like me."

"Arcadia—"

"Oh shut up brother dear! I've only been using you, never really cared for you."

"Oh shut up already. The princesses will deal with you when the time comes. In the mean time, take a nap." Luciana waved her hand and looked at Daniel who's skin had begun to take on a sickly green colour as his face contorted into dismay.

"You didn't know," asked Corbett.

Daniel shook his head. "I can't believe . . . why would she do that?"

"Power, everyone with no morals will succumb too power, whether it be good or bad," stated Luciana.

"She's my sister, I have—"

Luciana was shaking her head. "No you couldn't have done anymore than care and love, there is nothing more you can do. They are who they are."

He stared at her hatefully. "It's a hard concept to acknowledge."

"Life itself, is not easy," she said plainly.

There was a silence and Corbett stared admirably at his longtime friend. Luciana was far too wise for someone of her age.

"Your friend can have her room," said Daniel finally, looking away.

"Thank you."

After a short time, everyone was there and Esmerelda and Trixie had taken Arcadia out for interrogation. The room was quiet for a long time. Everyone ate in silene and just sat around. Suddenly Esmerelda and Trixie walked in. Daniel took tem in and stared at the blood on Esmerelda's clothes.

"Esmerelda, what did you do," asked Luciana.

"It was Trixie. Your sister attacked me, tried to turn me and kill me. Your sister had been turned like other we have seen. There is no magic that could have saved her."

"I am sorry Daniel," said Trixie bowing her head. "This is a tragic loss, but her mind was lost, forsaken to the darkness. She was dead long before my arrow hit her. I am very sorry." A tear fell down her cheek.

Daniel stood there silent gripping a chair. Luciana stared at him with Corbett ready to counter any spell he would say. But finally he spoke.

"No, it is as you said, she was already dead." He turned and looked at Luciana and Corbett across the room concerning. Luciana directed Corbetts glance towards him as he approached them.

"You two are the leaders correct." They looked at each other and smiled.

"We are," said Corbett.

"Then I would like to accompany you. I need to avenge my sister, destroy the monster who turned her into that abomination."

"You are more then welcomed too," said Luciana smiling.

"Do you ever think about her Daniel?" she asked into the mirror, waiting for him to appear.

He suddenly stood at her side staring into the mirror. "From time to time, she was mad, a talent that is most admirable now."

"It's a pity then that her bones are lost in the winds. It would have been nice to see her fight off Trixie, don't you agree?"

He laughed a cold chilling laugh and tapped the glass.

"Entia look across from you. That's your granddaughter, my daughter."

They watched as she looked up and smiled a sinister smile that only they saw.

"How soon till we pay them a visit?"

"Very soon," answered Luciana smiling.

Chapter Twenty-Six

Corbett stared out his window. He stared out at the black castle before him. He was going to have to kill her soon, or let her kill him. He would much rather die then have to kill her. He—

"Hello Corbett."

He turned around and faced her. Her eyes were their natural jade colour and her face wasn't malevolent but sad.

"Luciana—"

"Yes?"

"What are you doing here?"

"Paying you a visit of course, what else would I be doing here."

"I don't know, you've always worked in mysterious ways." Corbett did not smile but she did and her eyes twinkled.

"Of course I do."

"What are you up to?"

Her eyes turned their blackest and her smile was no longer sweet. "Your destruction. Just wait and see Corbett, you will lose, I guarantee it."

She vanished before Corbett could utter another word and stood there alone on his window sill. He looked out and saw Líead walking alone and in the dark. She stopped feeling his gaze and looked up, smiling at him. He smiled back and she laughed, a song like laughter that tantalized him, and ran off. He smiled and decided that he would follow. These woods were not a good place for any of them to be running off alone.

He slowly walked down the stairs. Everyone was staring at him and he began to wonder what he had done wrong. Trixie looked at him frightened and

Isabelle looked slightly angry. Donovan didn't even bother making eye contact with him as she held his great granddaughter.

"What?"

"They remember," whispered Trixie frightened.

"What!?"

"How could you be so stupid," said Isabelle shoving him. "You let your stupid affection get control over you! You idiot!"

"Donovan was supposed to erase their memories!"

"I did," he said defensively.

"So why do they remember? Everyone just started remembering."

"When," asked Trixie.

"Sometime last night after they had some drinks."

"Líead!"

"What about her," asked Isabelle.

"I haven't trusted her ever since she said Silkas name. I think she's a spy. I know it, she must have put something in the drink when you weren't looking. Where is she?"

"She ran off," said Corbett. "She was walking and then she smiled up at me and ran off."

"We have to go after her." Trixie bolted leaving everyone to follow.

Selene slowly walked down and followed all te people as they ran. Something was up. She ignored the few people remaining and ran after. She needed to see Edel.

Corbett quickly caught up to Trixie and was running alongside her. Coryn, Donovan and Isabelle followed quickly at their heels. They were nearing the edge of the forest and Corbett didn't like that. Líead was a trap. He knew he should stop, but he couldn't.

His feet pounded on the ground faster and harder. He needed to know exactly what was happening.

Finally they all saw her at the edge of the lake. Her hair flew behind her and her eyes seemed distant almost frightened,.

"Líead," called Donovan. Líead turned around and stared at him blankly. Luciana appeared followed by her generals one by one on either side of her.

Selene heard Galen call for Líead and shoved her way through the throng of people who had suddenly stopped. She soon saw why. There stood Luciana, in all her dark glory. She walked ahead, slowly toward Edel.

Donovan grabbed Líead and held her close.

"You witch what have you done to her."

"Oh, Galen is it, I have done nothing.

"What?" Líéad shoved Donovan away and took a step away and Selene looked at her as she stared at them hatefully.

"Líéad how could you," cried Selene.

"Oh this was easy," she laughed.

"Líéad how could you betray us," questioned Donovan.

Entia looked at him hatefully. "Because what kind of a father abandons his daughter." Donovan eyes glazed over.

"No."

Entia sneered at him. "What's wrong daddy, don't you like to play." She snapped her fingers and her disguise vanished into thin air and all that was remained was General Entia, Donovan's beloved lost daughter.

Finally Corbett knew what Luciana was doing. His fist clenched. Entia walked across the trickling river and Luciana did the same. Now she was closer to Corbett, she was closer to all of them.

"My, my what a group we've got here. You know I think that your comrades should get to know the real you, don't you agree."

She looked at Corbett than at her sister.

"Hello sister, how are you today."

Selene looked at Isabelle who was glaring at Luciana.

"Isabelle?" Isabelle didn't turn and look at her, she couldn't face the pain, not now.

Luciana looked at the princess then became distracted by Corbett. Finally the moment she had been waiting for.

Corbett knew what was about to happen and braced himself. This was something he could not prevent.

"Hello Corbett, how are you?"

Selene looked back and forth between them. She couldn't believe it, and more importantly she wouldn't.

"Edel, what is she talking about?" Corbett couldn't look down at her, he couldn't bare to see the anguish in her eyes.

"Edel!" Luciana laughed. "No wonder I was unable to see you! You switched your name with Coryn! Oh you are clever Corbett, you anticipated my moves."

"Edel!" screamed Selene.

Corbett wanted to kill Luciana more than ever. He hated her. Selene hated him and Luciana hated him. Two he loved despised him. Luciana walked up to him and gripped his face. He let her.

"What's wrong Princess Selene, didn't you know Edel here is *my* dear Corbett. Isabelle is my sister and Nathaniels ex-lover. Donovan is Entia father and that girl he's holding is his great granddaughter and Entia's granddaughter and General Daniels daughter. Trixie is General Esmerelda's sister and Coryn in General Nora's brother. Oh I could go on and on but I think I've overwhelmed you enough." A disfiguring smiled covered her beautiful face.

Corbett snatched his face away and Lucian's nails cut into his skin. Selene saw his cuts heal instantly. Her eyes widened and she took a step back horrified.

"No, It can't be true, it just can't be."

"Selene," said Corbett reaching for her.

"NO! You lied to me! You—you caused all this!"

"Selene please."

Luciana laughed harshly. "This is far too brilliant." She turned and walked away and an arrow shot through her. Selene looked at Isabelle and couldn't believe the hatred that emanated form her eyes. Luciana, however evil, was her sister.

"Oh sister dear—"

"Shut up."

"Why should I. Oh don't worry your secrets are safe for now. As you have said, they would never believe *me*." Isabelle looked at Selene who was looked at her frightened. Selene was her plan, she was going to use Selene to expose her and that was something she would never allow to happen.

Luciana pulled the arrow out and threw it towards the ground as she stepped into the river. She stared at her sister and knew what exactly she was thinking. Time to run away Princess she thought.

"Ah sister, how I do enjoy your presence." She turned her back to them. "Well have fun while you can." She vanished but her laugh lingered.

"Selene—" began Corbett.

"No, Edel, Corbett, whoever you are, you lied to me and betrayed my trust."

"Please let me explain."

"No!"

Isabelle knew she was about to run and looked at Toad who didn't look comfortable with the idea.

"Selene—"

"NO!" She ran off.

"After her!" Ordered Isabelle. Toad and a few other chased after her. Corbett looked at Isabelle worried. Isabelle was full of cruelty as she looked at him blankly then turned on her heel and walked back to the tavern.

"Selene, please be careful."

She ran and wouldn't stop but they were following her, chasing her, catching up to her. She needed to get away, run away.

"I'll grant your wish."

Selene stopped and turned slowly. There stood Luciana. She would have screamed but General Nathaniel grabbed her from behind.

"Ah, ah, ah, it's time to sleep." She snapped her fingers and Selene tried to fight to immediate flow of fatigue that flowed over her, but sadly, to no avail, she soon fell asleep.

Chapter Twenty-Seven

Selene woke in a cell with her hands shackled. She wasn't alone. Before her stood Luciana and all her Generals except Entia. She smiled sadly.

"She's replaced me hasn't she?"

"For the time being. I do plan to send you back, killing you now would be stupid. After all, you will die anyway, all of you."

"Why don't you just kill me now then?"

Luciana smiled. "I enjoy watching Corbett in pain."

"You are evil."

"You'll soon discover the reason for why I am the way I am. You'll find that things aren't always as they seem."

"I think I've already learned that."

Luciana laughed venomously. "So you would think." She bent down and her cold porcelain hands gripped Selene's face. "I am going to tell you a story and you are going to listen understand?" She jerked Selene's head up and down for her. "Good, we have an understanding." Luciana let go and sat back in a chair she summoned.

"Now, once upon a time there lived a girl who had a little sister and a best friend who grew up into a thief. This girl was the daughter to a family of mages and she learning magic and surpassed even her family. Her parents were overjoyed but sad because their younger daughter would always run away and never learn. She scorned magic, or so they thought.

"Now, the girl fell in love with the thief and when his Dark Majesty came they combined their talents and fed their town. They helped their town. But

172

then the plague came and his parents died while hers survived, So he swore he would stop him. Of course the girl wouldn't let him go alone and she they ventured off with a few friends.

"They walked and met many new friends. Soon after almost a year of preparing they, those fifteen friends finally arrived at his palace. They ventured in and attacked but the girl was captured because she saved the thief. He swore he would come back fo her but he never did and so for days, weeks, she was tortured both physically and emotionally. He showed her the truth that she would not believe. So one day she killed him and escaped and soon found herself face to face with the man she loved, kissing the princess forgetting obviously that he had promised to save the girl he had just ask to marry!" Luciana's grew wide in anger as she lost some of her composure. She quickly regained it though after a few fast breaths and sat back in the chair, wiping a lose strand of hair out of her face.

"So she gave herself to the darkness and hid away got centuries, preparing for the final battle." She sighed. "I hope you enjoyed that story because it always sends chills down my spine."

"Your presence does that all in itself."

Luciana simply laughed. "Oh I am going to enjoy everything I put you though."

"Which will be what?"

"Everything I endured. All the pain I felt, you will feel."

"There's more to this, I know there is."

Luciana simply smiled. "I am going to show you everything. If you come to the realization that everything I show you is true, when I'm done, the chains will vanish and you will be set to go. Oh and don't worry, services that weren't provided to me will be provided to you."

"So when do I get to leave," said Selene frightened as Luciana began to walk out.

"When I'm done of course." She walked out happily. Soon, Corbett, you will be mine, soon you will be mine to love, mine to kill, before you kill me.

*   *   *

Selene watched the door close. Corbett please save me, she thought. Suddenly she screamed. Something was striking her back. It was burning, ripping her apart. She wanted to fall unconscious. She wanted to pass out but couldn't. He had kept her conscious as she had tortured Luciana. He had kept her alive.

For hours this went on and Selene was in tears. What pain what horrible pain. Why had he tortured her, what had been his purpose.

The door swung open and General Nora entered alone with a tray of food. Her face stared down at her in disgust.

"How amusing." She set the food down and sat on the summoned chair. Selene stared at the food then back at her ancestor.

"You might as well eat. She doesn't have to feed you, she herself was barely fed. The food isn't poisoned, there are after all easier ways to kill you if that's what you're thinking."

Selene ate. Even after hours, the synthetic torture made her hungry. She wondered how Luciana survived.

"I simply cannot fathom why she is fascinated with you."

Selene swallowed. "Have you asked her?"

"Of course."

"Why did you allow this?"

"Allow what?" hissed Nora.

"The Darkness to overtake you."

Selene heard her growl. "Revenge. I was the first born, the kingdom should have been mine, of course my stupid brother had to be born. He snatched the kingdom, my kingdom, away from me! If I can't have the kingdom, no one should!"

"So you hate your brother that much?"

"Yesss."

"I love mine."

Nora sneered. "Do you now. Even after he tried to kill you in cold blood."

"She's twisted his mind, I don't blame him, or her. I blame whoever is truly responsible."

"And who do you think is responsible princess."

"Corbett."

"Oh how wrong you are," said Luciana. Selene stared at her as she walked in clad in her armour. Her cape flapped behind her. No symbol marked her like the others, instead it was plain, yet it made her marvel over her. This was the girl that Corbett once loved and deep down Selene knew that he still did.

"So you don't hate him?"

She sneered and placed her black nailed hands upon her bare hips. "No, I hate him, and I will continue to do so. He let himself fall prey to magic. His love should have kept him focussed! He should have come back for me!" Selene wanted to hide. Luciana's eyes burned with a rage that made her want to hide and die.

"I—"

"Say nothing, anything you say will be pathetic and mean nothing." Selene remained silent and just stared up at her. "Nora, is she done?"

"I presume so. The synthetic torture gave her quite an appetite."

"She's lucky I feed her." They looked down at her with penetrating gazes that made Selene feel as though she should die. So this is their power. Wherever Luciana went the world stilled, everything went numb, cold, dead.

"Stop please."

They sneered. "I don't think so." They walked out and left her alone.

*   *   *

The torture continued. She felt everything Luciana had endured and marvelled at her strength. She should have died, not lived. Her final torture had been her hand. It had almost ripped her apart and something had been inserted and burned there. The pain and shock should have killed her, the pain should have.

All those visions as well broke her. Her sisters betrayal. Corbetts promise. All the laughter. They all forgot about her. Isabelle . . . she betrayed her sister and killed the man she supposedly loved.

The door swung open and in entered Luciana followed by Entia and Nora.

"Hello Princess."

"What happened to your hand? You should have died."

She laughed. "I thought so too." She pulled the glove off her right hand and there embedded was crystal.

"What—?"

"A stone of immense power. Now tell me, what have you seen?"

"Everything. Your sister, Corbett, all of them."

"And now I will send you back. After you see one more thing."

"Please—"

"It would be best if you stopped. You will watch this."

"Can you please at least tell my brother that he had a sister once and that she loved him."

Luciana looked down at her and her eyes turned to a jade green.

"I will do that." She walked out and locked the door. "Nora, tell Albin that he used to have a sister."

"Why?"

"Just do it," she snarled. Nora flinched and obeyed.

Luciana was at the edge of the forest and looked in. Everything started here and would end here. She changed her appearance and walked to the tavern and turned the knob. When she walked in everything went silent. Corbett wasn't there and so she supposed that he was in his room.

"Selene," said Isabelle as she began to ascend up the stairs.

"Leave me." Isabelle did and she walked to Corbetts room. It took her a minute before she entered the room. She turned the knob finally and slipped in. He looked at her as she locked the door.

"Selene—"

"Please, just, I need and answer." He quickly walked over to her and kissed her. Luciana savoured it for a moment before pushing him away.

"No! Corbett do you love her?"

He stared ta her for a moment. "No."

"But you did, once."

"Yes, once, but no longer." Luciana smiled.

"Do you love me?"

He cupped her face. "Yes." Luciana's skin tingled the spell needed to last just a little longer, she needed to stay calm for just a little longer. They stared at each other and his hand went down to her waist.

"Do you love me?"

"Yes," she muttered faintly, losing her breath. He kissed her passionately and held her close. Just a little bit longer she told herself. Her cloak came off, then his shirt and their shoes and when he was kissing her neck she ended the spell.

Corbett felt a wave of magic and opened his eyes. He looked at Luciana's black coal eyes and pinned her down.

"Where is she?"

She laughed bitterly. "Oh don't worry, she's alive, I promise you."

"Your promises mean nothing to me." He gripped her longer and her eyes turned green and her nails faded in colour. Then suddenly her eyes were brimming with tears.

"Your promises meant everything to me."

"Luciana—"

"So you don't love me? You only love her?" He loosened his grip and cupped her face.

"Luci–"

"No, let me go!" She shoved him off her but he pulled her back and kissed her.

"Corbett—"

"I'll always love you Luci."

She kissed him lovingly and soon enough no more words needed to be said, nothing needed to be said.

*　*　*

"CORBETT!!" screamed Selene again and again. Nora smiled pleasantly at Selenes screams. Luciana was making her watch as she and Corbett made love. As always a very brilliant twist from a brilliant mind. She could hear her sob and scream and yell and she smiled.

"Finally, an heir."

Chapter Twenty-Eight

Corbett listened to her rhythmic breathing a she slept in his bare arms. He stroked her hair and let her sleep as he lay awake. He feared that if he slept she would disappear. He just wanted to run away with her, grow old with her, marry her. He took his pendant and put it on her. He wanted her to have it, maybe in battle it would save her from herself.

"Is it dawn?"

"I thought you were asleep."

"I thought you would leave me."

He smiled. "I would never leave you." Nails dug into his skin and Luciana gripped his neck and sat on his chest.

"Yet you did! You stabbed me! Thought I would die alone! You left me once."

He tried to pry her nails out of him but he couldn't.

"Luci–"

"Don't call me that," she snarled. Her eyes turned to coal. He kept his eyes focussed on the pendant. He could feel the crystal in her hand hard against his skin.

"Let me go." She did and moved off the bed. He snatched her by the hand and pulled her back planting a kiss on her.

"No!" she said as she pulled away. "You can't fix everything with a kiss Corbett! You can't repair all the pain!"

"Luciana!" He jolted up and held her against the wall. "Luciana please." He could feel her tears against his skin and she collapsed in his arms.

"You left me."

"I know."

"You asked me to marry you."

"I know."

"You–" He kissed her tenderly and cupped her cheek. She slapped him and stood straight. He stared at her.

"Luci–"

"No!" The wind blew hard and cold and the sun began to rise and reflect off her bare porcelain skin. Her nails as black as her eyes had become and that all to familiar evil smile came upon her face.

"Enjoy these few hours Corbett, it's all you have left before I destroy you." She vanished and Corbett stood alone in his room. Something dawned on him and he quickly got dressed. Selene, he . . . Corbett stopped with his hand on the doorknob. What was he going to say, that he slept with Luciana. He couldn't do that. He turned around and kicked his bed in frustration. What was he suppose to do. They couldn't rush in, especially because Selene was going to be sent back.

*   *   *

Selene's chains unhinged and she wiped away her tears. She could hear Luciana coming. Her boots and armour clanking as she walked. She came alone with food and drinks and summoned both a table and some chairs.

"Sit."

"You're–"

"I know I'm evil, but what can you do? Nothing." She took a sip of wine and Selene stared at her plate.

"I know how to stop you, how to end this curse on you."

"Do you really now, and what are you going to do about it? Are you going to tell Corbett, or Edel rather?" She laughed.

"No."

Luciana stared at her curiously. "And why not?"

"Because it won't do any good. It wont end anything. He needs to discover it for himself."

"Hmm, I doubt he will, even after six centuries that would be a miracle."

"That day you screamed and poisoned Trixie, he was close wasn't he?"

"No, the elf Cade was. I meant to kill him, not poison her, but it worked in my favour anyway." She took another sip of wine. "You should eat, we have a big day planned," said Luciana happily sarcastic.

Selene took a bite of food and made herself swallow it.

"I know you carry his child. I'll tell him that, they should know."

"Be my guest."

"I will tell them about Isabelle's betrayal. Only because they deserve to know."

"I expected nothing less from you."

"I have faith that Corbett will discover how to kill you."

Luciana laughed harshly. "Faith is a stupid word, I'll ask you not to use that word around me again."

They ate in silence and Selene held back her tears. Corbett had saved her, been around whenever she needed him. She loved him, but although he loved her in return, he loved Luciana more and always would.

Luciana jerked her eyes up. There was a certain type of darkness that just grew. Lucianas' skin prickled as it flew around. She smiled. She wanted this power.

'So princess, have you had your fill? Are you ready to go back?"

Selene nodded. "Yes."

"Good." Everything vanished and like a snake Luciana grabbed her arms and gripped it tightly. In a blink of an eye they were at the entrance to the tavern.

"Corbett! Sister dear! I've got something of precious value to you!"

Corbett jerked his head and ran down the stairs. Isabelle beat him out and they both stood with Coryn, Trixie and Donovan. Corbett looked at Selene who's gaze was attached to the ground.

"I told you I had something of yours."

Isabelle stared coldly at her sister. She hated her, Selene would expose her, if she knew the truth. They could not be afford to be divided. Isabelle silently prepared her bow. She shot at Selene but Luciana caught it an inch before her face.

"Bella, how cold. Is that how you treat a friend?"

"We don't know if it is Selene," she said simply, swearing.

"But I am Isabelle," said Selene keeping her gaze towards the ground, keeping her tears hidden.

Luciana let her go and people started coming out, started to watch.

"I can't—"

"Isabelle that's enough already, it's Selene dammit!" He rushed over to her but she shoved him away.

"Don't touch me! You—all of you have been deceived! Isabelle! Look at her, she betrayed you all! It's her fault all of this is happening! What is worse Corbett, the betrayal of love or that of a sister?"

"What are you saying Selene?"

Selene was crying. "Isabelle cast a spell six centuries ago, after Luciana was captured. She didn't want any of you to go in and die! She was being selfish!"

Luciana vanished but remained watching.

Corbett couldn't believe his ears. That was why he was unable to keep his promise. Otherwise he would have gone back, or died trying. His future wife, the one he would have grown old with. The love of his life . . .

"What?!" He was fuming, angry. He walked over to Isabelle who stared at him frightened.

"Corbett please, listen."

He couldn't help it, he slapped her and knocked her against a tree. She stared at him frightened and clutched her cheek.

"I was going to marry her! I would have rather died than live like this! I promised her I would go back for her! I LOVED HER!"

"Corbett please, if I had known—"

"Why should knowledge have anything to do with it! She was your sister."

"How dare you," said Donovan. "I lost my daughter and the woman I loved! How could you! You ruined hundreds of lives!"

"Nathaniel knew and she killed him because of it," whispered Selene.

Trixie walked over to her and slapped her. "How dare you Isabelle! She was our friends, she deserved better than this?! I lost my sister because of you!" She slapped her again then collapsed into tears in Donovans' chest.

"My sister," said Coryn. "My heirs, my people, have all suffered because of you Isabelle. How could you? And Nathaniel—he was going to tell us and you killed him, like you would have Selene." He stared at her, eyes full of hate, his face wrung in disbelief.

"Please you have to understand—"

"There is nothing to understand Isabelle," said Corbett sombrely. "You betrayed us and now what is there left to do?" He turned around.

"Corbett wait," said Selene, "there is something you should know."

He looked at her. "Yes."

"She made me watch and now she carries your child."

"What," said Isabelle.

"That wasn't me last night and he knew it. It was her."

"Selene—"

"Say nothing, for something good came out of it."

"What?"

"I know how to save her . . . and how to destroy her."

"How?" asked Isabelle eagerly.

"I wouldn't tell you." She looked up and stared at Corbett in the eyes. "I can't tell you Corbett, it is something you must discover for yourself." She walked away hugging herself.

"Can you kill her now Corbett?" asked Isabelle.

He looked at her hatefully. "How about I leave that to you *Bella*, you did it once." He walked away and soon found himself at the lake where he proposed.

"Hello there *Edel*." He turned and stared at Entia.

"*Líead*."

She laughed and walked over to him. "How are Cade and Selene?"

"Leave them alone."

"Why, will my father kill him like he did Silkas? I know Isabelle will take care of Selene." She glared at him. "Well Corbett, what is your opinion?"

"Cade won't betray us and if he does, Donovan won't do a thing. As for Isabelle, if she harms Selene in any way I'll kill her myself. I already ache to."

"How touching." She leaned her chin on his shoulder and her nails played on the back of his neck. He ached to hurt.

"What do you want."

"Just to thank you. You did save me that night by the well."

"I saved you from nothing."

"True, but I was trying to show my gratitude, however false. Now can I ask you something?"

"What?" he said agitated.

"Have you decided what to name your child?" She vanished but her laughed lingered. Luciana has his child. She had tricked him, he thought he wouldn't kill her, but he would. He'd kill her, he knew he would.

Chapter Twenty-Nine

As the dusk soon arrived they all knew that they were as ready as they would ever be for battle. Isabelle explained to them all they would be outnumbered twenty to one, assuming her sister did get rid of half a talon or two just to play with them.

Grey and black clouds covered the sky as they always did, looking down at her sweetly and Luciana smiled as she unclipped her cloak. She looked in the mirror and there he came. She welcomed his added strength. She tied her hair back and wiped away the lone tear that had frozen on her cheek. She would defeat him, she knew she would. She would kill him before she let herself die, but she would possess the princess first and smile down at him with her body in mockery and hatred.

Entia sharpened the tips of her arrows and sword. Her father would pay for all the hurt he caused her. For the abandonment, for the murder of the man she loved. When she was satisfied she wiped down her sword, Silkas' sword the one he gave her as he died. She would make him pay.

Damien circled about the castle floor. He would love to kill Trixie. She wouldn't marry him because he wasn't of the damned royal blood, of no noble blood, even though she claimed to have loved him. He would kill her because if he couldn't have her, then no one should, and no one will.

She had killed her brother once, or at the very least had tried to. But Corbett had to interfere and stab Luciana, giving life to the blessed curse. Nora would kill her little brother again and then she would take the joy and kill Selene and take the crown that should have been hers so very long ago.

She had betrayed him like he was nothing, like he had meant nothing to him. Nathaniel prepared his arrows, examining each tip as he coated it with his special poison he made just for her. He would shoot her through the heart and through that of her new lover. He would watch as they died apart and he would enjoy every last bit of it.

His daughter was his pride and joy. She was timid and shy but powerful and beautiful. Daniel would take her and kill her then make her his apprentice. Of course Entia would have to draw him away if Adira did not. He strapped on his armour and pulled out his sword.

Adira had watched her brother die. Silkas had just but followed his love as love deems necessary. He would follow her to death and die if need be. Donovan though had killed him in cold blood and she had seen the whole thing as he just let him fall to the ground. Entia had reached him first and he had died in her arms crushing her whole world, breaking her heart. She would kill him, and avenge her brother, she swore she would.

Esmerelda had gone back for her kingdom, but her sister had told a bitter lie. Esmerelda wasn't dead but reborn with a new . . . perspective on life. But her sister had stripped the kingdom from her. Trixie had always wanted to rule and when the chance arose she had taken it. But now all the elves were under her control, they were hers to rule and her sister could do nothing to change that.

Jason and Lucas sharpened their weapons. Such an array of weapons they had at their disposal. Isabelle had teased them all through their lives saying she would marry one of them. She always promised she would. She of course then always turned them against each other and fought one another to her enjoyment. But then she left them, abandoned them and scorned them. The only bright side was the fact that they hadn't ended up like Nathaniel.

Coryn knew that Nora would come for him. She hated him, always would. The kingdom would have been hers, if he hadn't come along. But he had and all her training had been for nothing, and he knew nothing about sword fighting. He practised and practised. This time he wouldn't have to take care of himself, he had to take care of Selene.

Knowing now who the father of his great granddaughter was he had to save her. He knew Daniel would try to take her and convert her, and he knew that Daniel was counting on both Entia and Adira to distract him just like he knew they would come after him and kill him.

Trixie sat in silence in her room. Her sister would try to kill her as well as Damien. She had hurt him and scorned him and her sister, she knew she had always wanted to rule, but not at the expense of her sister. Not like that. She sighed and wiped away her tears as she grabbed her sword.

Isabelle knew what she had done had been horrible but she had thought that her sister was dead. No, she had hoped she was. Luciana had always been the perfect child, and although she had resented her, she had loved her nonetheless. They were after all sisters and she had always looked after her like a big sister should. As before, she knew she had to fight to the death, even if it was her sisters.

Corbett stood alone amongst the old battle field. Here is where it would happen again. He didn't need to prepare for battle. He'd fight Luciana alone. She would come for him, and all among them, everyone would leave them alone. He would kill her, he no other choice.

Chapter Thirty

Luciana walked down the stairs and with a wave the doors opened. There her army stood. She walked through to the front lines. There stood her ten generals all with welcoming smiles on their faces. She returned the smile and looked up at the darkening sky. A snap of her finger and lightening flashed in the distance. Thunder resonated through the air. This would be the end.

Corbett could feel them coming, her vast army. Rain sprinkled on his face and then poured. Luciana had always been theatrical. He waited and soon saw her army with her at the forefront. At her sides were her generals. Her army wasn't as large as it once had been. Twenty to one. He pulled out his sword and braced himself.

"What a great army Corbett. You've got friends and family all around you." He gripped his sword harder. "You're not my family."

"No, I guess not." HS paused briefly and stared at him hatefully. "CHARGE!" Her army charged and Corbett braced himself as his people ran forward. He looked around for Coryn and the others and they were nowhere to be seen. They were off fighting their battle, like he should.

Nora hunted for her brother as she knew he hunted for her. She saw him holding Selene close by. She growled and searched around for Albin. There he was defeating all who stood in his way. She rushed to his side and snatching him away.

"Do not waste your strength on them, come with me."

"Why?"

"The witch. We're going after the witch." Nora ran through people, knocking over those that were in her way.

"Hello sister." She turned around and easily blocked him. A sneer crossed her face.

"Hello brother." She wanted to slaughter him. She stuck a blow but he was holding her off. She was beating him down but suddenly he tripped her. Nora gasped for air but quickly recovered.

"Is that the best you've got dear brother?" she said looking up at him, sneering.

"No."

"But it's the best I've got." Selene struck her but Nora kicked her in the gut and her wound quickly healed.

"You pathetic princess. You think you can stop me!"

"Yes."

"Please, I am the best warrior here, only Luciana matches me. What makes you think that you can stop me?"

"The simple fact that unlike you, I will be queen and was always trained for it." She swiped but Nora blocked her and battered on.

"It's a pity."

"What?"

"That your brother is going to kill Coryn and not I."

"Coryn!" Selene turned and Nora knocked her down.

"As before pathetic." She walked away and smiled at her brother who was ready for her.

"Hello witch." Selene looked up and above her stood her brother. "Get up and fight me."

*　　*　　*

Donovan took a few breaths while he searched amongst them he held both of his swords knowing full well that both Adira and Entia would come for him.

"Hello daddy, lets play." She lunged at him but he blocked her. "You damaged me."

"I thought I was doing what was best." She went for his head but he blocked it. A splitting sense of pain stuck his back. Adira, he knew.

"Hello love, how are you."

Donovan stumbled back to regain himself. He looked up at Entia and Adira as they stood together. Adira and her flowing auburn hair and piercing hazel eyes and his daughter with her flame red hair and purple eyes. He should have known that Líead was his daughter.

They both lunged at him. Entia wanted him to suffer. He may think he has but he hasn't, not until her sword went through him.

Adira wanted his head on a pike. He killed her brother and for that she would make him pay.

*   *   *

Trixie waited for the pair of them as they walked toward her. She didn't want to fight them but that didn't matter, nothing she wanted mattered.

Damien could see her and he wanted to lunge at her. Esmerelda drew her swore and Damien followed suit. Trixie wanted to to cry, as she pulled out her sword. She had to defeat them, she had no choice.

Damien and Esmerelda ran towards her and she prepared to fight them off. This would be the end.

*   *   *

Isabelle killed as many as she could. The rain was making her hands slippery against her sword hilt. She would kill all of those who stood in her path. She had to kill Nathaniel, she had to. She looked at Toad who was keeping an eye on her as he fought. Then there he was staring at her. He stared at her and she drew her arrows. She would kill him. She let go, but instead of hitting him it went into Luciana.

"Nice trick."

"This one is nicer." She shot the arrow out of her hand and Isabelle swung to the side. Nathaniel was startling at Isabelles' side. He kissed her and her stomach turned. She shoved him away and looked back but Luciana was gone and Nathaniel was back at her side.

"What's wrong Bella, sick." She lunged at him.

*   *   *

Corbett waited on the outskirts of the battle. Suddenly there she was, in all her glory. Her sword was drawn and her armour shined. He hadn't seen her in her armour since that fateful day.

"Corbett."

"Luciana."

"How are you?"

"Fine."

"You're friends are getting slaughtered."

"We'll defeat you."

"So you think." She struck down at him and he parried her off. So this was it. He struck at her but she easily blocked him and smiled.

"Come and get me Corbett."

*   *   *

Coryn kept blocking his sister. It was all he could do to stay alive. It been so long and he was getting exhausted. The rain had finally stopped and the moon shone brightly. He needed to rest. He needed a break.

Nora didn't need to relax, she wanted him dead. She charged and hammered down on him. She would kill him. Her foot suddenly caught in something and she lost her balance.

Coryn took the chance to knock her down and battled Albin away snatching Selene. They needed a break.

Nora growled and Albin helped her up.

"They went that way."

"Lets head them off." She grabbed him hand and vanished to where Coryn was. "Did you really think you could run from me baby brother?"

"Not really." He struck and she struck and soon enough disarmed him. He took a step back, he had one chance to do this. Corbett hurry up.

*   *   *

Trixie was finding it difficult to keep her balance. She couldn't focus on it. She had to trip one of them to get the advantage. Sadly though, she tripped and fell back. Her weapons fell out of her hands as did her breath. She stumbled back and they both smiled. They brought their swords together and prepared to strike. So this would be the end. She closed her eyes and braced herself or the pain. When none came she opened and above her stood Cade, his sword holding them off. She took the opportunity to trip her sister and take her sword. Now they were even and she had one chance, her and Cade.

*   *   *

Isabelle fought him with unwavering strength. This wasn't Nathaniel, there was no way to save what was once her Nathaniel. She fought and fought. She wouldn't give in. She would not be the one to lose today. She tripped and fell and saw Nathaniels blade but suddenly she was snatched from the air and sat gasping. Before her stood Toad with Nathaniels sword protruding from him.

"No!"

Nathaniel jerked his sword free and Isabelle caught her lover. No, she couldn't lose him.

"Bella—"

"Shh."

"My name—"

"Toad please."

"It's Markus." She laughed and smiled and tears streamed down her cheeks.

"Markus, I like Toad. I love you."

"And I you." She kissed him and felt him die in her arms.

"How sentimental." Isabelle looked up and stared at Nathaniel.

"How dare you, I'll make you pay."

"You'll have to wait till I'm done making you pay." Isabelle grabbed Toad's sword.

*　　*　　*

Donovan fought off his daughter and his love. They pounded their swords against his again and again. He needed to defeat them in order to save them.

He sliced at Adira's armour. His daughter was his main priority. He got ready. Hurry Corbett he thought.

*　　*　　*

"You left me to die."

"I should have come back—"

"You believed that I was truly evil."

"I know what I did was a grave mistake."

"Hmm." She swirled and cut at his chest. He swore at her. He hated her, he wanted her dead. "You never loved me." She lunged at him and his eyes widened. He finally knew how to stop her. All the time her eyes were green, all those times she was herself, she wasn't really gone. Luciana wasn't really dead. He finally knew how. He loosened his grip and her grip faltered giving him the chance to drive his sword into her. He held her as she gasped, their faces touching.

"You think this can stop me?" She breathed as she felt the sword move through her body.

"Yes."

"Well you're wrong."

She pulled her face back and smiled at him. "And why is that?"

"Because I'm not killing you because I hate you . . . I'm killing you because I love you." Her eyes widened and he kiss her. He had to save her.

"Corbett—" Suddenly a scream shook the air.

*　　*　　*

Coryn took his hidden dagger and plunged it into his sisters heart. Nora simply smiled.

"Please brot–" She stoped and stared at him wide-eyed. "It cannot be."

An ear splitting scream shook the air and he caught his fallen sister. He looked at Selene who was cradling her brother. The un-dead fell dead and the curse on the elves seemed to be lifted.

*　　*　　*

Trixie quickly stabbed her sister in the heart. Esmerelda took a dagger and stabbed Trixie in the arm. She fell back and crawled away. Cade who was up against a tree took a dagger and planted it in Damien neck. He stumbled back and fell to the ground.

"No!" screamed Damien. A scream shook the air.

*　　*　　*

Donovan had but one chance. He ignored his daughter and concentrated on Adira. He quickly drove his sword into Adira then quickly grabbed her short sword and drove it into Entia as she came at him. She gasped and stared at him shocked.

"Luciana." A scream shook the air.

*　　*　　*

Isabelle grabbed Toads sword and drove it into Nathaniel. She could feel his sword in her side and so be it. If she had to die then he was dying with her.

"This won't—" His eyes widened and he walked off the blade. "Luci." A scream shook the air.

* * *

Her armour turned silver and her eyes turned back to jade. She slid off the sword and fell to the ground. Corbett caught her and held her close. The sky lightened and the moon shone brightly. He could see all around that the dark elves were no longer dark and he looked up. Isabelle stood far away tears in her eyes, clutching her side.

"Luciana."

"Hello Corbett." She coughed and blood squirmed out of her wound. Tears stung his eyes.

"Corbett do you know, I've always loved you."

"I've always loved you Luci."

"I know." She coughed again and a tear fell into her cheek. "Don't cry," she said wiping it away sadly.

He shook his head. "A healer. Someone get a healer!" Donovan took a step but a barrier blocked him.

"No! Corbett listen to me — you may have broken the curse but he still lives in me. I have to die—"

"No."

"Corbett my love, I have to." He held her close and could feel her smile. "Corbett look at my hand." He did and it pained him to do so. "This stone is a part of me, it's very powerful and it's keeping me alive for only one thing."

"What?"

"C–close your eyes." He did and he felt himself whisked away. When he opened his eyes he couldn't believe it.

"I wanted to comeback home Corbett." They were home at the lake, and the sun was rising. "I wanted to see the sun rise once more at home." He looked down at her. She was crying and dying in his arms.

"I love you Luci."

"And I you Corbett." The sun was rising and she smiled and looked at him. He kissed her and her hand touched his cheek tenderly. He held it there until suddenly it went limp. She was dead but the crystal glowed and he found himself back amongst his friends. He cried and cried and he held his dead loved one close to him. Her body was limp, she was dead. Luciana Sanluida was dead. His child was dead. The love of his life was dead.

"Corbett?" He looked up at Selene. "Corbett the elves are back to normal. They brought caravans on their way here and want to bring us home—with the generals—your old friends. I don't want to bury them here, I want to bury them at my palace."

He nodded and lifted up Luciana. No one would touch her, he killed her therefore he would carry her.

*   *   *

The road back home was a long one. Selene sat with Isabelle in the wagon that carried Nathaniels body.

"Why did you do it?"

"I thought she was dead. Hoped actually. All my life she protected me, would yell at me then tell me it would be all right. I never had control over my magical abilities so it scared me. My subconscious would control it. So I wanted to hide from it. Unfortunately it was why my arrows always hit their mark. I was hoping that if she was dead what I was doing would be okay.

"Corbett wanted to rush in there. Luci would have never allowed that. I needed a plan but nothing ever came to me. I wanted revenge for my sister not to sentence her to her doom." She stroked Nathaniels face. "I never meant for my arrow to hit him. I had no control over it. When I looked at him all my thoughts came rushing out. I was scared of what he knew, but I didn't want this to happen to him."

"I'm sorry for all that you've lost."

"It has all been but my fault."

Selene watched her and looked at the wagon behind. She could see Corbett stroking Luciana's face.

Epilogue

Corbett stood at Luciana's grave in the palace courtyard. It was beautiful how the roses blossomed. He was alone except for Trixie who came to his side.

"So what will you do?"

"Exile."

"Like Isabelle?"

"Yes."

I will be helping Isolda rule the elven kingdom. Coryn says he'll be here and advise Selene. Donovan is going to get to know his great granddaughter."

"I'll just wander."

"Do as you wish. I am going to say goodbye to Selene, I don't know when I'm going to see her again."

Corbett smiled. "Give me a hug." Trixie gave him a hug and kissed him on the cheek.

"Don't wander too far." She left him alone and he stared at Luciana's grave.

"Wandering does' become you my love." Corbett looked up and there above him stood Luciana.

"Luci—"

"Shh. Corbett I'm dead but I'll always be here. Just call me if you ever need me." She laughed but quickly became serious. "Live your life Corbett. You love Selene and she loves you. Don't waste your life wandering, living in the past, moping around."·

"I wasn't going to mope."

"Ah but you were." She smiled and they both knew she was right, as usual.

"I'll always love you."

"I know." She descended down to him and kissed him warmly, passionately. "I'll always love you." She took a step back and Corbett turned and walked to the palace. He did love Selene and he knew she loved him. He smiled and looked back. Luciana stood and said but a single sentenced, "we'll be waiting", and with that she vanished. Corbett smiled then turned back around, letting the door close behind him.

THE END

Get Published, Inc!
Thorofare, NJ 08086
25 January, 2010
BA2010025